Emma Jane's Guide to Matchmaking the Mayor

Drew Taylor

Taylor Made Publishing

Cover Design by Callie McLay

Interior Design by Drew Taylor

Edited by Leah Taylor

Proofread by Lindsay Rankin

contents

To Jane Austen.

Thanks for crafting stories millions upon millions of people have enjoyed. *Emma* might not be everyone's favorite, but it's my favorite. Thank you for writing a character you knew some people wouldn't like so others like me could relate and love her.

Emma Jane

RULE #1: DON'T FALL FOR YOUR CLIENT.

Weddings are supposed to be happy occasions.

Beside me, my father blubbers like a baby as my former nanny, teacher, and continual lifelong friend, Halle Taylor—soon to be Weston—states her vows to Grant Weston within our small venue: Hartfield Presbyterian Church.

I elbow my father in the side. "Papa. Pull yourself together. We are here to support Halle, not take away from her special day because you can't fathom her leaving us."

Papa sniffles then chokes back another sob at my mention of her leaving, but overall, he quiets himself.

I paste another smile on my face, quickly glancing around the small chapel packed tight with what I presume to be the entire town of Hartfield, Mississippi. We all sit on cushioned red tweed, wooden oak pews with red carpet underneath our feet. Dahlias line the aisle and red rose petals blend into the floor where the flower girl joyfully marched through about thirty minutes ago. The air is thick with stuffy perfume and the smell of flowers. It's perplexing to me that weddings also smell like funerals.

"You may kiss your bride," Reverend Philip announces, and Grant sweeps Halle into his arms, sealing the marriage with a sweet, tender kiss. The room erupts in masculine applause and an orchestra of swooning ladies.

Once the newlyweds turn their attention to their guests, Reverend Philip states, "Ladies and gentlemen, I present to you Mr. and Mrs. Grant Weston."

Round two of applause and swoon.

Except for my father, who seemingly can no longer control his cries.

"Papa," I hiss through my smile as I once again glance around us to make sure nobody is paying him any attention. Halle and Grant have already exited, so we should be safe. I know Halle; she would stop her wedding to console Papa.

He looks at me with saddened blue eyes. "Marriage is awful, Emma Jane. Promise me you'll never marry. First your sister. Now our sweet Halle."

"I'm only twenty-three. I'm not leaving you anytime soon, Papa." I place my hand over his, and he sandwiches it. The wrinkles in his skin are a reminder that I'm a product of a forty-year-old woman giving birth, and it's my fault I never had the chance to meet my mother.

Logically, I'm aware I'm not the sole cause of my mother dying while giving birth to me, but I've always felt the need to make it up to my father and older sister somehow. Remaining behind to take care of my father in his advancing age while my thirty-four-year-old sister, Bella, galivants around England with her husband, Gerald, seems like the perfect sacrifice to make.

Mostly because it isn't that much of a sacrifice. I'm perfectly content to live in our three-story Antebellum home, graciously using my father's money (and the little I make working as a barista at Books and Beans in the neighboring college town of Juniper Grove) to fund the necessities I need to survive while pursuing my recently discovered true calling.

"Oh, Emma Jane. What a lovely and superb match you made between these two." I look away from my father's hands to see Mrs. Jane Austen, a long-time family friend and as well-on in age as my father, standing before me. Releasing my father, I stand to embrace the woman I was partly named after. Emma came from my mother and Jane came from the woman who is, for all intents and purposes, my second mom.

"Ah, yes, well, the moment Mr. Weston waltzed into our home at my asking and laid his eyes on Halle, I knew he was a goner. When he left, she talked to me all night long about his dreamy brown eyes and perfect cheekbones." I chuckle, remembering that occasion only three months ago. Frankly, I thought three months was too short a time to meet and then marry, but to each their own. The two of them obviously fell in love at first sight.

Jane laughs, tossing her head back while strands of silvery-white hair fall from her bun. A hand rests on her flat stomach. "Cheekbones? My, what a unique thing to notice about someone upon a first meeting." Watching her laugh, I'm overjoyed at the liveliness the woman carries. For sixty-five, Jane is vibrant and youthful. I hope I'm like her when I get to be that age.

Glancing at Papa still sitting in the pew beside me, the joy fades. He is the opposite of vibrant and youthful at sixty-seven. Raising two girls on his own, well, with the help of Halle after Mama passed away, while also trying to successfully run the family business passed down to him by his father, took its toll on him. He did it, of course. And he did it well. But it's all catching up to him now...

"Yes, well, they are pretty sharp."

"Indeed, Emma Jane. Correct as always. Have you made any more plans for starting your own match-making business?"

My heart raps with excitement. "Yes! Tons of plans. You should see my office back at home. It's filled with vision boards, books on the subject, and I even have a list of potential clients!"

"Brilliant! I know you'll be highly successful. Our perfect little Emma Jane can do no wrong." Jane claps my shoulder then turns her attention to my father. I preen under her adoration and attention for one moment, but then a pit settles deep in my stomach at the phrase *can do no wrong*.

"Oh, Henry. Didn't you just love the wedding?" Jane asks my father, who only makes a noise—something akin to a growl, huff, and snort rolled into one. Jane backhands him on the shoulder. "Henry. Don't you be this way. You know good and well Halle could not stay with you forever. I know she's like another daughter to you, but she's forty. It's time she settles down."

Papa locks his eyes with Jane, and the hot end-of-July air chills. *Okay, it's time to go.*

"Let's get going," I say, using both hands to tug Papa by his arm off the pew. He obliges and stands of his own free will. To Jane, I say, "Knightley comes home tonight, right? Do tell him to stop by tomorrow for dinner. That would surely lift Papa's spirits. You are more than welcome to join us for our Sunday meal as well."

Jane's blue eyes twinkle. "Of course, dear. But you know I love my bingo on Sunday nights. I'll send my son over with a tray of my famous cowboy cookies. How's that?"

I beam. "Perfect, Jane. I love you. Bye for now!" And with that, I'm dragged out of the church by Papa, even as people stop to congratulate me on a match well made. It's been a while since Papa has moved this fast; he seems more than ready to leave the scene of the crime.

I mean the wedding.

"Knightley, son. Do come in." Papa shuffles across the dark wooden floor of our home, his bright red slippers flapping with each step. I busy myself lounging with a book on the dusk blue settee by our fireplace. Though it's the beginning of August, Papa has a fire flaming high and bright. He's always cold and swears there's a draft in our sitting room.

I silently wonder if Casper the Friendly Ghost haunts this antebellum home. It wouldn't be the first old house to boast the presence of a deceased entity.

"Did you bring the cowboy cookies? Your mother so graciously volunteered you to be the delivery man yesterday at the wedding."

Papa continues to pepper Knightley with questions regarding this last trip to New York for a mayor's conference. They chat in the dining area, speech sometimes muffled by what I assume to be the cowboy cookies taking up residence in their mouths. Knightley's deep, rough voice echoes throughout the Georgian style walls as he talks about his experience meeting President Marshall and his wife, run-ins with political powerhouses, and the corrupt bank-rolling scheme that is the lobbyist.

Tuning out the talk, as I'm sure Knightley will repeat it all in my presence later, I open my paperback copy of *Queen Victoria's Matchmaking: The Royal Marriages That Shaped Europe.* Though I read plenty of how-to books on the subject, the best source of learning is through the trial and error of those who came before me.

And what other perfect person to study is there than the matchmaking grandmother queen herself? It was an era of propriety, class, and womanly wit, after all.

Halle and Grant were such a success, and now I have my next target in sight: my friend Henrietta Bates, who works at Books and Beans with me. She's a lovely young woman from south Mississippi who can do much better than the man she's currently crushing on. She simply needs a little push in the right direction, and who better to provide that push than her very own devoted and loyal friend who has all the connections and societal standing needed to ensnare her a good man with money and status?

"I hear congratulations are in order as you are solely responsible for a marriage," Knightley says from behind me in a voice oozing sarcasm. He's biting back a retort about how my matchmaking schemes are inferior and unneeded, I just know it. A large, pale, freckled hand pats my head. No, I can't see it, but I know this man better than I know my own image in a mirror. That includes his looks AND his unsavory personality.

Correction: his only-unsavory-for-me personality. Everyone else gets a friendly, though commanding, impression of him.

"I accept your kind compliments, Knightley. Though even I recognize I could never accept credit for a marriage between two consenting people." I hope he hears the causticness in my tone. This is how all of our frays begin. We speak in false niceties until one of us breaks and speaks our true thoughts. That's when the real fun begins.

No one goes toe-to-toe with me like Knightley Austen, the only person in this small, uppity town who doesn't seem to care if he hurts my feelings or speaks against me. He says what he says, and he never bothers to take it back.

Knightley doesn't treat me like I'm glass. Like I'm motherless.

He used to not be so calloused, however.

It wasn't always this way. He used to help me solve puzzles, do complicated paperwork like college applications, and he encouraged me to get a business degree. But over the past two years, he hasn't quite liked my business ideas. First, he shot down my therapy-horse-riding-for-kids idea. Then, he shot down my online boutique idea. Now, he's going to shoot down my matchmaking idea.

Knightley harrumphs, his large frame moving between me and the fireplace, blocking the waves of heat wafting from the area. His auburn hair is loose and unkempt, the curls he usually combs down sticking every which way. The trimmed beard that matches his hair is tamed and covers half of his face, enhancing his baby blue eyes. They shine brighter than the water in the Bahamas where I took my high school graduation vacation five years ago.

Objectively speaking, Knightley is one of the most handsome men I've ever seen, but that's neither here nor there. He's thirteen years older than me and was once married. He's my brother from another mother, so I can in good conscience speak to his handsome looks while acknowledging it means absolutely nothing in terms of romantic interest.

"The entire town seems to think it's your doing." He sits down on the chair opposite me, tugging at the dark wash jean fabric around his upper thighs, and continues. "I've heard 'Emma Jane did a wondrous thing for Halle,' and 'How generous of E. J. to set up dates for Halle and Grant,' and 'She's starting her own matchmaking business, haven't you heard?'"

"And if I were?" I tilt my head, gauging his reaction. He maintains a perfectly placid expression; the only sign of misgiving is the twitch of the corner of his lips, barely noticeable if I weren't examining his face like a spy locked on her target.

Knightley folds his hands in his lap as he crosses one leg over the other. "Then I would advise you to reconsider your business endeavors. Attempting to launch a matchmaking business in a small town like Hartfield, Mississippi, is begging for failure."

I cross my arms and sit straighter, rolling my shoulders back. "Just because I launch and operate from Hartfield does not mean my skills will be contained to this area. There's this thing called the internet, and it comes with several gems like social media and websites."

"What experience will you flaunt? Will you brag about matchmaking your former nanny and teacher to the local dairy farmer? The same man who was already interested in Halle but too shy to act on his desires?" Knightley's condescending tone coupled with a sharp, raised brow that says "got you, Janie" has me throwing my chin in the air and looking away from him as if I can't even stomach giving him the time of day.

"Everyone starts somewhere. I'm twenty-three. I have time to build my empire, Squire. You can help or get out of my way." He rolls his eyes at my nickname for him. I stand abruptly, brushing down my plaid pleated skirt that ends mid-thigh, and head toward the dining room where I'm assuming Papa is still stationed, taking his fill of cowboy cookies.

Footsteps echo behind me, but I don't grace the incorrigible man by acknowledging his presence. "How did Jane do with this batch?" I ask Papa right as he is brushing crumbs from his green polo shirt.

"Delicious as always. Though I'm certain every batch gets tastier and tastier." Papa beams, gazing upon me proudly as if I were the one who baked and brought the cookies over, before he glances beyond me. "Please tell Jane that she is outstanding as always."

"Of course, Henry." Knightley sidles up beside me, the top of his shoulder taking over my peripheral vision. "She will be thrilled to hear your praises. Speaking of praises," he pauses, and I stiffen, "the town is alive with talk of Emma Jane's new business venture.

How do you feel about our girl starting a matchmaking firm?" He throws his arm over my shoulder, tugging me against his side.

Papa begins to remark on how excellent it is that I'm pursuing this path, so long as I don't get myself married, while I try to wiggle out from underneath Knightley's arm. He's basically got me in a chokehold at this point, but both men talk back and forth about the logistics of *my* business as if I'm not right there caged within a stupidly strong arm while I fight to pry my way out of the encompassing scent of spruce and vanilla.

Finally, I cease my efforts, feigning defeat in the hopes that he will loosen his grip enough so that I can bolt. My father gives Knightley a strange look at that moment; it's an expression that seems to be reminiscent of Alice from *Alice's Adventures in Wonderland* where she cries, "Curiouser and curiouser."

Knightley coughs, yanking his arm off me as if I'd lit him on fire, then takes three giant steps sideways, creating a chasm of distance between us.

I'm not complaining one bit, but even I have to admit Papa's expression was weird and Knightley's response was weirder.

I smooth my hair down and adjust my off-the-shoulder, scalloped, red crop shirt back into position before reaching for a cowboy cookie. I take a bite, the sounds of my chewing filling the silence. Papa still has that strange expression as his eyes linger on Knightley, and Knightley has taken to twiddling his thumbs and looking everywhere except in Papa's and my direction.

"Okay, guys. What's going on?" My question jerks Papa from his trance-like state, and he smiles softly at me.

"Nothing, dear one. I would love to hear more about your matchmaking plans. Why don't you go grab your materials and then meet Knightley and me back in the sitting room?"

My gaze bounces between my father and the massive redhead in the room, questions buzzing around my brain. But Papa is interested in my budding career, and even better, he's going to force Knightley to listen to my epic plans. Surely this will win the Negative Nancy over to my side.

I take another cookie before leaving the room and bounding up the creaky stairs that lead to my room. I don't need Knightley's approval, but it would be nice to have his support. He's been in my life ever since I can remember, and whether I like it or not, his approval means the world to me. It's why I fight him so hard when he pushes back against me.

Everyone in this town loves and adores me, and I'm well aware of it, but he doesn't treat me in the same manner.

And for reasons unbeknownst to me, he's the one I want to shower me with affection.

Emma Jane

The key to a successful scheme is to lay the groundwork before striking while the opportunity is hot.

I place the corner puzzle pieces quickly, then I begin working on the sides. "You know, Henrietta. Frank Weston, Mr. Weston's son, is down from New York for a month. Word is he's still single. Maybe I can set something up." I raise my eyebrows at her before continuing my puzzle.

My friend, with her short, curly brown hair and doe brown eyes, sighs. "E. J., he's *Frank Weston*. He's loaded with money and lives in New York. There's not a chance in heaven he'd be interested in a plain, orphaned farm girl such as myself. First it was the son of the Mississippi State senator. Now an investment banker who doesn't even reside in the state. Why do you keep trying to set me up with men so far out of my league? And men that would eventually force me on a plane? You know I refuse to fly."

I purse my lips, placing the last side puzzle piece for the 5,000-piece image. I think this may be my fastest time yet. "You have a warped view of yourself, Henrietta. Or you severely lack confidence." I stand, tugging her with me. I walk her over to the stand-up mirror in my bathroom and play with her hair. "Look at yourself. Your milky white skin is without blemish. Your hair doesn't frizz. You are not in need of makeup or jewelry. How could any man turn you away? You will not have to get on a plane, and if you do, then you'll be so in love that you'll feel safe. Will you trust me?"

She turns her soft expression to me. "You mean it?"

"Yes, Henrietta. I mean it. Will you do as I say with Frank Weston? I have a plan, but you must follow it to a tee."

I stare into her widening eyes. She swallows once and then nods.

"Good." I smile and then return to my puzzle on my wooden table that I've devoted entirely to puzzles. As I search for a faded green piece, I go over my outfits in my closet, mentally picturing her in each of them until I land on the right option. "Henrietta," I sing her name, "I have just the outfit for you to meet Frank Weston in."

She groans, running her fingers through her brown curls, which bounce right back into place somehow. It's her personal magic trick, I'm sure of it. "Please do not put me in a sequin skirt and silk top."

"I—"

"Well, a silk top would be okay. But no sequins. Or lace." Henrietta takes my hand between hers. "I'm not you, E. J. Don't try to dress me as if I'm your favorite doll."

Her request takes me by surprise, though I guess it shouldn't. I'm used to people copying my style in this town but looking back, Henrietta has never been that way. Maybe it's why I keep her close?

"I just want to see you happy and thriving within this small, debutante-centric society."

She gives me a pointed look. "You forget I wasn't a debutante. That was you."

"But you were there for me through the entire process. You might as well be one." I smile, removing my hand from hers and bounding toward my walk-in closet. Regardless, I want to make her look and feel like a high class woman. "What's mine is yours, Henrietta. Now, allow me to show you my idea. If you detest it, then we will look through my other clothes."

The next hour is spent switching between various fabrics, neckline cuts, and statement pieces. Henrietta grumbles and groans but finally settles on a red long-sleeve silk blouse with a long cut from the shoulder to the wrist. She chooses a high-waisted, flowy white skirt. Then I force her to wear simple golden hoops with diamonds on the bottom, matching bracelets, and a necklace.

"E. J., why am I fully dressed in this getup right now and why are you doing my hair? I was under the impression the meeting would be later in the month..."

My lips twitch. "I never said that, Henrietta. You assumed. Frank Weston is on his way over as we speak. In fact, he should be here—" The doorbell rings, and I rock onto my toes with delight. "Marvelous. Let's go win you a keeper."

"Emma Jane! Wait—"

I grab her wrist and yank her behind me, momentarily cursing myself for not making sure her toenails were painted since we don't wear shoes in the house. *That's not being perfect, E. J. Do better. Details matter.*

"Listen to me, Henrietta. Be your charming self. Smile softly, laugh at his jokes, tuck your hair behind your ear, and bat your eyelashes when he compliments you. Understand?" I pull her through the third-floor hallway, down the winding staircase, and through the first-floor hallway until we reach the edge of the sitting room where my father, Frank's father, Frank, Halle, and... Knightley?

What's he doing here?

"Ah, Emma Jane. Come in," my father says in an overly cheerful greeting. "Look who's here. Frank Weston." He catches Henrietta at my side, promptly noticing how she looks ten times better than I do right now as I sport an oversized hoodie, leggings, and unwashed hair. Unfortunately, I'm the type of girl who will steal the show, and I don't mean that to be conceited. It's simply a fact, and I have lost many friends over it. Therefore, I opt to dress down—even though I love dressing up—when hanging out with other women who are single. I don't have evidence that Henrietta would be that way. In fact, I believe the contrary, but it's happened too many times in the past for me to even risk it.

"Henrietta Bates, please come in. Have you met Frank Weston?" My father manages a small smile and an awkward nod toward me, letting me know he's onto me and what I'm planning. The lights in the sitting room are off, so only the glow of the fireplace illuminates the cream walls with their golden siding.

I grin, thinking about how good it is to always have him on my side and in my corner even if he isn't quite on board with marriage. I glance at Knightley as Henrietta and I walk into the room, and his expression is far different from my father's warm, approachable demeanor. Knightley frowns, his eyes shifting between me and my friend. He obviously knows what I'm up to as well, but where my father is encouraging despite his disdain for marriage, Knightley seems as if the idea of my matchmaking Henrietta with Frank gives him a stomach ulcer.

As we exchange greetings, I'm not subtle in my attempt to size Frank up. While shaking his father's hand, I notice Frank is tall and lean, sporting chocolate brown hair similar to his dad's. Though unlike Mr. Grant's, Frank's hair is thick and lush. When I embrace Halle in a tight hug, I catch sight of Frank over her shoulder sporting an easy smile with crinkles around his dark eyes.

Then against my will, as I'm attempting to watch Frank greet Henrietta, two large hands wrap around my biceps from behind, spinning me around until I'm face to face with the current thunderous rain on my matchmaking parade.

Face to chest, I should correct.

And I scowl at that broad expanse, refusing to meet his stormy blue tornado-cloud eyes that will hail down disapproval.

"What do you think you're up to, Emma?" Oof. He single-named me. *Big mistake, buddy.* I finally lift my eyes, jutting my chin.

"Whatever I so please, Knightley George Austen. So stay out of my way and go ruin someone else's fun."

He releases my arms, one hand resting on his jeaned hip while the other runs through his auburn hair. With an exhale, he proclaims, "You can't run around meddling in the lives of others. Frank and Henrietta? Really? What are you thinking?"

I fold my arms across my chest, meeting his stare and cocking out one hip. "I'm thinking it's a match made in heaven. Look at them."

I glance over my shoulder to find Frank pulling out a spare chair for Henrietta. He catches my gaze and nods once, wearing a pleased smile.

"See?" I whip around toward Knightley while my thumb points at the obvious love blossoming behind me.

"Do you even know what kind of man he is? Why he's back in Hartfield? And think about Henrietta! This is real life, Emma Jane. Not a romance movie where the poor girl gets the hotshot New York man."

"He's a perfect gentleman for Henrietta. And would you look at her?" I turn around again, this time maneuvering to Knightley's side. "She's got that whole girl-next-door vibe with her wide, almond-colored eyes and simple style. Any man would be a twit to not fall in love with her."

Knightley's warm breath tickles my ear. "Then, pray tell, Emma Jane, why does he keep side-eyeing you?"

"He's suspiciously eyeing the man hovering beside me like an annoying fly."

I move to stand behind Henrietta, effectively deciding to photo-erase Knightley from this scene. Frank Weston sits across from us, chatting with my father. Grant and Halle sit on the gray ornate loveseat together, gazing into each other's eyes as if they didn't just get back from their three-day honeymoon.

Henrietta twirls her thumbs in her lap, nervously looking at Frank and then back at her fidgeting hands. Time for me to intervene.

"Frank, it's so good to see you here in Hartfield again. I feared you'd disappeared on us for good. How's life back in New York?"

Conversation between Father and Frank ceases as both men acknowledge me with pleasant smiles. Frank clears his throat, man-splaying in the settee before resting his elbows on his knees. "New York is full of life, character, and... stimulation. You would love it there, E. J."

"Henrietta, haven't you mentioned before that you were just dying to see what New York looked like outside of the movies?" I place a hand on her shoulder while I fix my gaze on the still-grinning man. "Frank, why don't you show us pictures of the Big Apple?"

He stands abruptly, and I register his tall, looming frame beside me in seconds. I adjust myself so that he is forced to lean beside Henrietta.

I nudge her arm from the other side, and she pivots her head in my direction. Good. He should catch a whiff of her light floral perfume. When she looks at me with concerned eyes, I encourage her with a smile and a tilt of my head in Frank's direction, where he has already whipped out his phone and is scrolling through his camera roll. As he begins to show us pictures of the city, Henrietta comes alive, shedding her nerves and stepping into the lovely, down-to-earth woman I've grown to know and admire.

By the time I edge away, the two of them are laughing, making pleasant conversation, and immersed in talks of urban life compared to rural life. I finally allow Knightley back into my frame, tossing a smug look of "told you so" in his direction, where he still hovers at the bylines of the room like a gothic hero awaiting to insert himself where he doesn't belong.

I waltz over to him while humming to myself, and when I'm near enough, I stand on my toes and ruffle his hair. "See? I know what I'm doing, Squire. Don't doubt my abilities again."

He sighs in a tone that says *I'm-so-over-you, Emma Jane*, pinching the bridge of his nose. "Do you have a sick, sadistic wish to see your close friend suffer?"

"*Pft*. What are you going on about?"

Knightley glares at me, searching for any hint of understanding. When I raise my eyebrows, he runs his hand through his hair, turns his back to me, and then immediately spins to face me again, leaning down so that he's inches from my face. "Frank Weston is here because he went bankrupt in New York. He's manipulating his father into selling the family farm and land. And here you are trying to set a pure, innocent soul up with the devil himself."

My brain doesn't compute, and I continue to search his eyes for any detection of deceit. Knightley, however, has never been one to lie no matter how impossible he can be toward me. "Why is that not reported in the news? I did a thorough internet search on him days ago when I learned he was coming down. No one has even whispered about this."

"Do you think every single investment banker on Wall Street is reported about?" Knightley laughs without mirth as he stands to his full height. "Frank's a big deal, but he's a small-town big deal. Not a national big deal."

We both snap our attention to the gasp coming from the other side of the room. Henrietta is on her feet, staggering backwards from where Frank is kneeling down beside the chair she was sitting in.

"I can explain..." he says before drifting off then standing and turning to face me.

"He has pictures on his phone, Emma Jane." Henrietta's disgust rings deep as she points an accusatory finger in Frank's direction. "Of nude women! Doing *things*."

"And there's reason number five thousand and fifty-four that Frank Weston is a rotten soul," Knightley mumbles under his breath.

The room is blanketed with quiet, only the crackling fire breaking the smothered silence.

Frank laughs stiltedly, bouncing his gaze from his father to me and then beside me to Knightley. Then, a slimy smirk snakes across his face. "I'm a twenty-six year old self-made man." He shrugs as if that excuses his actions.

"Self-made, my—" Knightley curses. I watch as his naturally red-tinted face turns to a deep maroon as anger engulfs him. "Grant, do you know why your son is home? Truly?"

Grant's wide eyes flicker to his son. "To celebrate my marriage?"

"He's here to take your farm from you and sell it to the highest bidder back in New York. He's broke, Grant. Not a penny left to his name. Your son is as corrupt as they come on Wall Street."

"You have no idea what you're mouthing off about, Knightley." Frank's booming voice is full of rage. "How dare you accuse me of such actions."

Without retaliating, Knightley walks to the corner of the room, grabs a manila folder from a side table, and brings it to Grant. Hesitantly, Grant takes the folder from Knightley and pulls out a hefty stack of papers. After several prolonged moments of papers flipping, Frank protesting, and Father sitting in the corner with his nose in a newspaper, Grant stands.

"We will talk about this at home, Son." He takes Halle by the hand, says his goodbyes to all of us, then leaves.

"I think you should follow them out," I say, moving to stand beside Henrietta, who still looks shell-shocked.

"I will happily escort you," Knightley says, already approaching Frank. Frank snarls and curses at Knightley the entire way through the hallway and out the door, and once we hear the click of the lock, Henrietta crumbles into my arms, a sob breaking out.

I pat her back as Father stands, likely going to look through the window to make sure everyone is good outside. I take advantage of the moment of privacy.

"Do you want to talk about it?" I peel Henrietta off my shoulder.

She shakes her head, wiping at the tears rolling down her cheeks. "Do you believe me now? That a girl like me has no business remotely entertaining a guy like him?"

"Henrietta, listen to me." I pat her cheek. "You are not at fault, okay? None of us knew—well, except Knightley—what type of man Frank Weston is."

"No, Emma Jane. I mean that he is awful and I am good. I want a good man. And while I know city men can be good, I prefer someone I know and closer to home. Someone I can easily vet myself."

"Noted." I let her cry on my shoulder as she mumbles about the images on Frank's phone, things I will never repeat. Father comes back into the room, stating Knightley followed Frank home and won't be back because he needs to tend to primary election matters. *At least I won't have to face his unbearable gloating.*

For a brief moment, I wonder how I could have been so wrong about Henrietta and Frank when my first match—his own father—was perfection.

Father's phone rings. "Reverend Philip. To what do I owe this pleasurable phone call?"

Reverend Elton Philip...

Local, single, handsome, kind, and well-known...

Wouldn't have abhorrent pictures on his phone.

"Henrietta, I've got a new plan."

KNIGHTLEY

RULE #3: CHECK TO MAKE SURE YOUR CLIENTS ARE TRULY READY TO BE MATCHED. DON'T FORCE SOMETHING THAT ISN'T GOING TO WORK.

Oscar Wilde once said, "To expect the unexpected shows a thoroughly modern intellect."

I must be a thoroughly modern idiot.

"How could this happen?" I ask the stoplight, the only one in this little town of Hartfield as I head toward my mama's place. All poll projections pointed in my favor for this year's mayoral primary election, but here we are, a neck-and-neck race between me, a Republican, and newcomer and Independent, Jansen Johnson, or Jay, as everyone calls him.

I run my fingers through my hair, no longer caring that I've ruined the styled look I sported earlier at my day job, Donwell Family Law, which is named after my grandfather, Donwell Austen. He's the one who encouraged me to pursue a degree in law instead of taking over the family's financial business. My brother, John, does a good enough job managing that, anyway.

His constant and unwavering support allowed me to pursue a life I love—practicing family law. I entered the political arena four years ago because no good candidates were running for office. Good people, sure, but not ones who could really make a difference in the town. More like old codgers who knew they could at least keep the status quo around here.

My job as mayor of Juniper Grove, Mississippi, Hartfield's neighboring college town, seemed secure. My first term went splendidly. I passed many affirmative legislations to make Juniper Grove a better city to live in by focusing on tourism, which is hard to come by in the Delta region of the state. I also amassed cohesive support between both Democrats and Republicans, and I even continued my positive work as the head lawyer at Donwell Family Law practice.

I was a shoe-in for re-election...

Until I wasn't.

Until *he* entered the race.

For once I wish this city held primaries for city elections.

The silence in the car is interrupted by an incoming call over the system.

Marcus Long.

"Hello, Knightley speaking."

There's a loud bang like an engine misfiring, which considering Marcus's workplace, could very well be the case.

"Sorry about that," he says breathlessly. "Just saw the news. Want to come over for pizza and beer in an hour? I'm about to close up shop for the evening."

The light turns green, and I rev the engine of my day car, a white Maserati, before speeding off, letting my frustrations out on the road.

Calm down, Knightley. The last thing you need is a speeding ticket. Then you can really kiss your second term as mayor goodbye.

Though sometimes, I wonder if I would survive a second term.

The people are good to me in this town, but those who are adamant I'm not qualified to be mayor of Juniper Grove are loud. Their reasons are: I didn't grow up in the town, I'm unmarried and therefore don't understand how to properly protect families, and, of course, those who despise Republicans. Though, to be fair, those are the ones I have the least encounters with. My most prominent opposition is from those who follow the local Southern Baptist association's new president, Pastor Vance Green, who I continually push back against for twisting scripture to fit his political agenda.

Whether I let people see it or or not, the constant pushback and workarounds do get to me. Especially when they accuse me of not being a true Christian because I don't interpret scripture the same way they do.

"I'll stop by Mama's place first, but yeah, that sounds like a good plan."

Not one for continuous conversation over nothing, Marcus hangs up. The rest of the ride home is uneventful, just me all up in my head and ignoring constant calls from my small campaign team. I do mean small. It consists of three people plus me.

After swinging by Mama's house to reassure her that I am, in fact, okay, I make my way a little farther into the sticks, until I find myself at the end of a mile-long dirt driveway staring at a simple but nice cabin in the woods.

A few magnolia and oak trees are boasting tall around the cabin, creating a good source of shade in the midst of the summer heat, but here in the dimming evening sun, it creates a sea of orange and yellow hues that even the best painter could never recreate as purely and perfectly as God is presenting the image in front of me. Shaking my head clear of the marvelous picture, I take the three steps that lead me into the quaint home. Log beams hold up the roof; wood covers the walls, the floors, and the cabinets. The matching maroon furniture breaks up the monotony of the light brown wood color. An unlit fireplace sits against the wall with a bare mantel waiting for pictures of a thriving family.

Cami, my deceased wife, once stated that no matter what home we settled into, she wanted a fireplace with a mantel to show off the amazing family we would grow together.

An idea that died alongside her in the cold expanse of Alaska.

"Right on time." Marcus rounds the corner holding two beers, and I smell homemade pizza wafting from the kitchen.

"Are you sure you don't have Italian roots instead of Korean roots?"

Marcus laughs, his monolid eyes crinkling in the corners as he hands me a drink before leading the way back to the tiny kitchen. "I'm a mutt. You'll never know 'cause Mama will never tell."

He's a shorter guy, though not small by any means. His past job as a farmhand and his current job as a mechanic shows. Plus, if I was to challenge him in a wrestling match, he would smirk and shake his head, knowing well and good he'd take me down within an instant. Marcus is a competitive mixed martial arts fighter, and he often competes around the state.

"If you're the mutt of your family, then I'd hate to see what your child will look like one day." I grab a slice of Hawaiian pizza topped with mushrooms and peppers before sinking into one of the two recliners.

Marcus joins me on the other recliner, then in unison as if we are Chandler and Joey from *FRIENDS*, we lift the side levers and groan in pleasure.

"That's the stuff."

I grunt in agreement.

"Wanna watch TV?" he asks.

"You don't want to talk about our day and make sure our emotions are in a good place first?" I hitch my eyebrow in his direction as he shakes his head and laughs.

When he clicks on the television and logs into Netflix, I notice his recommended shows and movies are chock-full of Korean dramas.

Marcus motions toward the TV and talks around a bite of pizza. "See? I don't need to talk about feelings. I watch these and remember I'll never get a woman anyway because I'm not the grumpy son of a rich CEO."

"Rich CEOs are not all that and a bag of chips, Marcus. What you have to give a woman is so much more."

My younger friend stares at me as if *I'd* just spoken Korean.

"Okay, yeah." I clear my throat and take a swig of my drink. "Moving on. Too mushy."

After a pause, he pops his neck then pegs me with a serious stare. "What are your plans moving forward in this election? Jay is already a popular person in Juniper Grove for his contributions to relief efforts when the Mississippi River flooded several years ago."

I release a slow breath and take a bite of pizza. "I don't know. Yeah, he helped with relief, and he's filthy rich. But I've made our town a real college town. People like to visit Juniper Grove now. When you look at Jay and me on paper, we are tit for tat on policy, promises, and procedures."

"Look at you sounding like a real politician with your alliteration. Or are you actually a Baptist preacher?"

"What's the difference between the two?"

We laugh as he continues to scroll through Netflix. I say the one thing I've been avoiding. "I think—" a pit settles in my stomach, and I breathe through it. "I think it's because he has a wife and kids, you know? People see that as 'more than.' Especially here in the south. If he can lead his family, then he can lead the city. He'll have Vance Green's support since Jay is actually a Southern Baptist and I'm not, which will take a lot of votes from me. But what I don't get is that I've been leading the city well for the past four years."

"Right," Marcus helpfully adds.

"I had a wife. God just didn't see fit to let me keep her past the honeymoon."

Marcus pauses his search and sets the remote down. "In all seriousness, do you want to talk about it? I know it's been eight years since the accident, but I also figure some moments of healing are harder than others."

The man can be articulate when he needs to be. "I'll always miss her, and sometimes I think about her when I least expect to think about her. But I'm okay. I've made peace with it. I just don't think marriage is something I want to try again. She was the one, you know?"

"Understandable," Marcus says. "So are you not going to try and even the score between you and Jay?"

"Ha. As if I'd find someone to fall in love with and marry before the election in November. Besides, it wouldn't be the worst thing if he won. He's a good man, and I think he'd continue to improve this town. And I don't plan on moving my church membership to Southern Baptist. I'm perfectly content at my Presbyterian church."

"It's three months. Stranger things have happened. I'm sure any woman would love to be the wife of the mayor. And you're a lawyer. That says a lot in itself."

I choke in disbelief. "Do you hear yourself, Marcus? Quit watching those ridiculous K-dramas, okay?"

He laughs then clicks on a particularly cringe-looking drama. "Trust me. Just watch one episode and you'll be hooked."

I stand. "Find a girlfriend to watch these with."

"Hm. Henrietta comes over occasionally and watches them with me. But I hear Emma Jane is matchmaking her with Frank Weston."

"You're late for town gossip. That's in the past, and Grant has already given Frank a job until he's back on his feet from bankruptcy. E. J. is attempting to match her with Reverend Philip now."

Marcus looks up at me from his seated position, the last bite of pizza at his lips. "What? The reverend? Is it... going well?"

"Seems to be, actually." I shrug, feeling that familiar taste of disdain on my tongue. Why Emma Jane feels the need to match people up is beside me. Her talents do not lie in matchmaking but in relational business. Sure, she could start a great business from this, but it's Hartfield, Mississippi, for crying out loud. Not the best place for a startup. She's too confident for her own good, too beloved by this town such that her ego is sky-high. I have thirteen years of life on her, and if I've learned one thing, especially today, it's that overconfidence in yourself will lead to your destruction.

But don't take my word for it. Pride is the downfall of man, according to scripture.

Reverend Philip, however, has been oddly open to Emma Jane's attempts to get Henrietta and herself in a room with him.

"Hm." Marcus stands, setting the empty plate down on the small end table between the chairs. "Is Henrietta receptive to his advances?"

"I couldn't tell you. In order to maintain cordiality with E. J., I've stepped back." Then it dawns on me. "You like Henrietta?"

Marcus shifts his glance down to his feet, then to the empty plate on the side table. "I said she comes over and watches K-dramas with me." He says the words as if the meaning behind them was obvious.

"Dude." I clap him on the back. How does one equate watching television together to interest? I watch television with him all the time. And E. J. "Why haven't you asked her on a real date?"

"I don't know, man." Marcus picks up the plate, and I follow him into the kitchen. "Emma Jane is trying to set her up with all these high-profile men."

I scoff. "Reverend Philip is not a high profile man."

"No," Marcus contemplates, "which is weird. Did Henrietta have a change in heart?"

"Do you think Henrietta is responsible for these setups?"

"Yes?"

I laugh, placing my plate into the sink. "Not a chance. This is all Emma Jane and her desire to launch a matchmaking service."

"In Hartfield, Mississippi?"

"My sentiments exactly."

Marcus is silent as he washes the dishes. I busy myself with putting away ingredients from his cooking. Finally, he says, "Do you think Henrietta would say yes if I asked her out?"

I think for a moment. I have honestly thought the two of them would be a healthy match. I've mentored Marcus for a long time, ever since he became a Christian years ago. We quickly became friends. In a small town like Hartfield, you befriend whoever you can.

I've caught Henrietta and Marcus admiring each other countless times, but unlike *someone* I know, I'm not trying to play God and make matches.

"I think so. She's only a few years younger than you. You have a steady job. She's got a good head on her shoulders." I grin and waggle my brows. "And you're obviously handsome. Why would she say no?"

With renewed confidence, Marcus straightens his shoulders. "Will you help me write her a letter?"

"Why a letter?"

"You know I suck at talking. I want to get this right."

A smile breaks across my face. "Let's go."

Emma Jane

Rule #4: Create healthy tension between your clients; some sparks won't light themselves.

"Emma Jane! Look!" Henrietta darts into my workplace, Books and Beans, which is a cafe-slash-bookstore in the neighboring town of Juniper Grove. She's waving a folded piece of paper in her hands, the smile on her tanned face impressive.

"Whatcha got there?" I polish off a mug and place it on top of the clean, disjointed stack.

"A confession!" The squeal in her voice reminds me of the joy I experience when I find the perfect accessory for an outfit I once forgot existed.

I snatch the letter from her hand as she holds it out to me. My blood runs cold. It's a confession, sure enough. A good one at that.

But it's not from Reverend Philip.

It's from Marcus Long, the local mechanic who grew up a farm-hand to the Weston's, like his father before him. I quickly scan the letter, noticing diction that echoes a certain tall, red-headed, pompous man I've known my entire existence.

Makes sense. I don't think Marcus could articulate this by himself. I glance above the letter to see a blissfully hopeful Henrietta shining full-moon eyes at me.

It would hurt her if she knew Knightley wrote this—and he will hear from me later—but more importantly, Marcus Long is not the man she needs. He can't give her the fabulous life she deserves to have. Henrietta was orphaned as a baby when both of her parents died in a tragic plane crash. She grew up with her loud and obnoxious aunt, Mary Bates, and was forced to work as a farmhand to Grant Weston. Which means she has definitely known Marcus for a long time, but I know in my soul that she deserves someone who can give her a better life. Not more of the same ole, same ole.

I gently place the letter on the wooden counter that separates Henrietta from me. Pasting a sensitive smile on my face, I begin. "Henrietta, you are my closest friend, are you not?"

"Yes." I don't pay attention to the way her face falls a decimeter.

"And you trust me to match you with a good man who can give you a good life, do you not?"

A centimeter. "Yes."

"Do you truly think Marcus Long could give you a good life?"

She brightens. "I do, Emma Jane. He's kind, honest, and hardworking. We've known each other forever. To be honest, I've always had a little crush on him, but we were friends, and I didn't want to disrupt that status quo. But knowing he feels the same way, well, it's thrilling, is it not?"

"An absolute twist of fate," I bite through my false smile. A teensy part of me whispers that I should let her have this. Marcus is a *good* man, no doubt, even if he often takes advice from Knightley.

Okay, Knightley is a good man, too. He's just impossible toward me, and it low-key hurts that he's a butt to me and not everyone else. But I guess that's what older and supposedly wiser family friends are for.

"For the sake of bluntness, Henrietta, I think you can do better. Marcus is a good person, yes. But I think you deserve a more fulfilling life than he would be able to grant you." I shrug and push the letter toward her, watching hesitation flicker across her face. "The choice is yours. I think you should give Reverend Philip an honest chance, but I will stand by you whatever you decide."

"So," Henrietta looks down at the letter now in her hands and then back up to me, "you think I should tell Marcus no?"

"I didn't say that," I emphasize.

"But I should give Reverend Philip a chance?"

"I think that's the honest thing to do since I've already set a date for you two." I tap my fingers on the counters, then someone walks through the doors, the wind chimes hanging above me dance and sing with the small wind route. "But the choice is yours."

She nods with determination. "I'll give the reverend a chance. That would be kind of me." Then as if she's made her conclusion, she squares her shoulders. "Yes. I will tell Marcus that I do not reciprocate. It was only a little crush. Nothing worthy of exploring."

Hm. That was a quicker turnaround than I was expecting.

"Thanks, Emma Jane. I'll see you later." Henrietta turns on her heel, walking out in a quick strut. Did her voice quiver or was that all in my head? My heart clenches with guilt, but I remind myself this is for her own good. She will see the wisdom in my nudging when the two of them fall madly in love.

"Hi, Kelly," I greet a returning customer. "The usual?"

The older woman smiles at me and nods. After paying, she goes and sits in one of the cushioned chairs near the bookshelves.

As I make her Christmas-themed latte, even though it's only the beginning of August, my mind wanders toward the possibility of someone writing me a love confession. Sure, I've sworn off marriage because my father needs me, and well, there's the little problem that there's a large probability I can't have children due to polycystic ovary syndrome. Fifteen-year-old Emma Jane was distraught when she learned about her PCOS diagnosis. I wouldn't want to put a man through the ringer of falling in love with me only to have him find out that I probably couldn't have his babies. That would shatter his heart.

And it's rare to come across a man here in the south that doesn't want a baseball team for himself.

That's why I keep my guards strong and high, constantly evaluating them for cracks and crevices. It's for the good of the world. I protect myself, and I protect any man who may want to get too close to me.

And Papa.

He would be helpless without me around.

I deliver Kelly her spiced latte then tend to another table who finished their lunch. My coworker, Kelsey, organizes books on the shelves. Stone Harper, the director of the Juniper Grove Community Center, was in here not too long ago and said we needed to restock Lucy May's, our local author, books. I placed the order recently, and I make a mental note to construct her own display when they arrive.

I have so many business ideas for this place.

For starters, I wish we could add lotus energy drinks to the menu.

Outside of that, I want to restructure the bookshelves to where they are embedded into the walls instead of in stacks. I want to place two little nooks in the opposing corners for people to sit and read in. Expanding the building would be costly and require a lot of work, but it would also create space for soundproof rooms where people who struggle with sensory overload, like my friend Lorelei, could come to just relax or study or simply be.

I think I could do great things with this place if Mr. Sam, the elderly owner who has a kind heart but stubborn will, would ever sell.

My phone buzzes in the back pocket of my ripped, high-waisted jeans. It's a text from Reverend Philip saying he has tomorrow evening free since he finished his sermon preparations today. I send him a quick reply, letting him know I've set reservations at Lakeview, a restaurant in Juniper Grove, since Hartfield has a grand total of zero. I don't tell him Henrietta will be the one meeting him there; I don't want to ruin the surprise. I haven't missed the way he eyes her during sermons. I nudge her every time he does, and she blushes and rolls her eyes.

Reverend Philip is a good-looking man with his pale skin and black hair. He has nice muscles, and he's tall. Like a vampire who has leaped straight from the pages of a morally gray romance.

Except the reverend has good morals. He wouldn't be in the position he is in if he didn't. He is a respectable man of God, and Henrietta will do well with him.

He texts back and says he is looking forward to his blind date, though I do wonder why he put the word blind in quotations. Oh well. I put my phone away and set to work wiping down tables, thinking of the various outfits I could dress Henrietta in tomorrow for the date. Lakeview has outdoor rooftop dining, which I need to go ahead and make the reservation for. It was a tiny white lie that the reservation was made, but all's well. It'll be made in a moment.

Once I finish wiping the tables down, I call and make the reservation and text the details to Henrietta, also telling her to come by my house two hours before the date. She probably assumes it's so I can dress her like she's my personal doll, and she'd be right, but neither of us acknowledge it.

Right as I put my phone away again, Knightley texts me.

Squire: Want to come over after work to watch a new movie on Netflix?

I smile to myself, appreciating the moments where he's like this. He probably feels bad for berating me so harshly about my business endeavors, so he's making up for it with buttery popcorn, virgin margaritas, and boxed candy. It's a new thing we've started doing over the past couple of years. It started when I was stressed out from one of the finance classes I was taking, so he distracted me with a movie night before helping me out with the class material.

That led to a fight over whether my expensive clothes could be considered assets or not. To apologize for arguing with me when my clothes could in fact be assets if I started an online boutique, he turned on another movie and called it his apology movie.

Me: Yep. But I request food.

Squire: I'll pick something up for dinner.

***

"You wanted to watch this?"

I stand beside Knightley's big screen television, pointing to the absolute monstrosity of a movie. There are literal monsters with big teeth on the preview reel, and it's dark in his living room. Not my jam...

"I thought this was an apology movie," I mutter under my breath, knowing full well he can hear me. He didn't mention we were watching a horror film as we chatted over Mexican takeout.

He sits down on his long, black sofa and tosses a handful of popcorn into his mouth, chewing it up and chasing it with a sip of his virgin strawberry margarita before setting the drink down on the table end beside him. He responds. "And pray tell, dear Emma Jane, what do I have to apologize for?"

Sometimes I think he just likes the way my name sounds coming from his condescending mouth.

"Putting down my business, mocking me for the whole Frank Weston thing, always being an absolute turd to me."

He raises his auburn eyebrows, the perfect match to his styled hair. "Turd?"

"Yes!" My voice is a little too loud and a little too flustered. Bringing it down, I snap. "You are so nice to everyone else, but you are a turd to me."

"Then why did you agree to watch this movie with me, Emma Jane?"

"Because I thought it was an apology movie," I hiss under my breath.

He pats the plump cushion next to him—my usual spot when we watch movies or shows together—and I reluctantly sit down, crossing my arms like a petulant child.

Next thing I know, Knightley's breath is tickling my ear. "What if this actually is an apology movie? What if I chose horror instead of romance just so I could watch you *need* me for two and half hours?"

I blink once. Twice. A million times. "Excuse me, Squire? Are you a sadist?"

He chuckles, shaking his head. "Not in the slightest, but I do *so* enjoy getting under your tanned skin."

My cheeks heat, and I turn my head away so he can't see my blush.

Why in the heavens is Knightley George Austen making me blush? I guess if anyone would have said something like that to me it would stir the butterflies in my stomach to take flight.

After a breather, I turn toward his smug face.

Smug... *everything.*

His arms are crossed against his chest, pulling the thin fabric of his pastel blue button down shirt taut across admittedly defined muscles. His dark blue eyes are narrowed as his expression rivals those Matt Rife memes floating around the internet. Smug and confident and oh so superior looking...

What's the best way to take him down a notch or two? And make him blush harder than he made me?

"Oh, for heaven's sake, *King*." He snaps his head to look down at me. *Good.* "You couldn't handle being under me."

Someone behind us clears their throat, and I snap my head behind me as Knightley mutters a curse under his breath.

"I let myself in as I usually do," Marcus says with suspicion dripping in his voice. It's not like he hasn't seen me at Knightley's side plenty of times, but we've never given off the vibe that's clearly suffocating everyone in the vicinity.

As Knightley stands to address Marcus, I fly off of the couch and announce to the world I'm going to go pee.

Real classy, I know.

Once I've locked myself in the bathroom, I splay my hands on the marbled counters and stare at my pinkened reflection in the large mirror above the sink. What is wrong with me?

Knightley knows how to get under my skin, sure, but it's never been like *this.* Flirty. Charged. A touch of forbidden.

In fact, I've *never* felt the feelings he's curating in me before. Not even with the two guys I dated momentarily in college just to experience the hype. Spoiler alert: Both relationships tanked quickly when I told the guys I wasn't sexually inclined.

I'm second guessing that now. What's with the tingles and flush and butterflies? It's throwing me off my game, and I need to toss these ridiculous notions out of that double-paned window by the porcelain bathtub.

After cooling my face and ridding myself of nonsensical thoughts (like Knightley is intentionally flirting with me and is not just trying to tease me in a different manner than he usually does), I make my way back to the living room just as the front door shuts.

"Marcus left," he says, stating the obvious and acting like nothing happened. "Ready to watch the movie? Here," he grabs a box of Whoppers from the end table, "mix these with the popcorn."

"But this is my apology movie. I shouldn't have to get butter hands," I state, crossing my arms. If he wants to act like we didn't *flirt* with each other moments ago, then so be it. Probably because he didn't mean anything by it and I'm being a twit.

"Not an apology movie, but think what you want to. It's still your turn to mix the goods." He sits down on the couch, man-splaying in his khaki pants, as he opens the box of candies.

I huff and roll my eyes, but I sit down and grab the popcorn from the brown coffee table in front of us, then he dumps the Whoppers into the bowl. I slip my hand inside and gently coax the popped kernels of corn out of the way so the candy can fall to the center and bottom of the batch.

"If this isn't an apology movie, then what are we doing here?" He gives me a napkin to wipe my hands off with, but I will most definitely be making a bathroom trip to wash my hands in a moment.

Knightley shrugs, pressing play on the movie. "I wanted to see this."

"And you couldn't have watched it with Marcus or some other friend?"

He looks at me with a cheeky smile, his blue eyes stark in the dim room as the bright screen reflects within them. "You are my friend, Janie." Then he does the unthinkable and ruffles the top of my head. "And I should treat you to horror films occasionally."

It's on the edge of my tongue to ask, "Then why in a million lifetimes would you say you want me to *need* you and then say you like getting under my skin? My *tanned* skin?" But I don't ask. Instead, I click my tongue at him for messing up my perfectly curated Hollywood waves and head back to the bathroom to wash my hands. Who cares if I miss the beginning of this atrocious movie.

Once I'm in the bathroom, I allow myself one more itsy bitsy moment to fall to pieces over Knightley's unprecedented attention. It's... new. I don't know where it's coming from. Maybe it was all in my head. Lord knows he jokes with me, but where did the flirtiness come from? Is it because I am currently surrounding myself in the study of romance and love for my matchmaking business? Yes, that must be it. My head is full of nonsensical ideas that only work for other people and not me. I'm projecting, and I need to take Taylor Swift's advice and calm down.

And then I remember what I said back to him, and I slap myself on the forehead with my freshly washed hands. "Way to go, Emma Jane. No wonder he messed with my hair and spoke to me like I'm a little kid. He was reminding me of a clear boundary that I danced right over with my comment about him being...

"Oh, God. Why, why, *why* did I say that? It was completely inappropriate in the first place, not to mention I said it to *Knightley!*" My thoughts continue spewing out of my mouth in a prayerful plea. "He can't handle being underneath me? Gah! What was I thinking? Please, if You can give him amnesia, I'd be eternally grateful."

I take a steadying breath and then walk with confidence like all is well in the world. Knightley doesn't say anything to me, only hands me the popcorn so I can try some. We continue in silence, and when a grotesque creature pops up on the screen, I pull my knees to my chest, thankful I wore jeans to work today instead of a skirt, and mentally prepare myself for the nightmares that are sure to follow based on the sounds from the movie alone. Yeah, I've officially shut my eyes, and they will remain squeezed shut through this entire thing. Which begs the question: Why didn't I just go home once I realized what movie he wanted to watch tonight?

I don't know the answer, but as a loud, screeching sound sends me jumping over into his body for protection that's not necessarily needed, and he holds me tight against him for the remainder of the film, only releasing me once the credits roll, I have suspicions I stayed because bickering with him is my favorite thing to do.

Even more fun than barista-ing.

Even more stimulating than matchmaking...

Emma Jane

RULE #5: BE FLEXIBLE AND ABLE TO SHIFT PLANS. HUMANS ARE MESSY.

I tap the ballpoint of the pen to my temple, brainstorming ideas about how to make the next date better.

"He complained the entire time about the food, the art on the walls, and then at the end of the night, he didn't even tell me goodbye." Henrietta paces my room like an early spring tornado, a force to be reckoned with, as she recounts her date from last night with Reverend Philip. "He stood, snorted, and walked out of the restaurant. At least he didn't leave me with the check..."

"See, there's a plus!" I smile, but even I know this isn't a good look for the reverend. Maybe he was having a bad night?

Henrietta stops in her tracks, and I'm positive a trench now divides my room in half. "You call that a plus? That was the least he could do after treating me like I wasn't there for most of the evening. Seriously, Emma Jane. I think he asked, like, one question about me. The rest of the conversation, if you can even call his ranting that, was centered around him or how nothing met his expectations. I think he was disappointed it was me there and not you."

"Nonsense," I interject. "He was probably too flustered to act right around you. Men lose their sensibilities in the presence of a pretty woman. I've seen the way he looks at you in church. He's definitely interested." The looks he gives her during the sermons sometimes border on creepy, but he's over our church, so I don't doubt his intentions. Though if what she's saying is true, maybe I should.

Henrietta takes to frustrated pacing again as I put down my pen and set to work putting together a puzzle to calm my nerves and redirect the part of my brain that needs to be actively doing something to think appropriately. The puzzle is an 8,000 piece English landscape, and I might have to frame this one. "Give it one more date next weekend, okay? If he acts like that again, then we will call it quits. But I'm banking on the fact that you flustered him and his inner immature boy came out."

She's quiet for a while as I continue my puzzle, but then she sighs and agrees. "The best part of my night was running into Marcus afterwards. Well, it was weird since I rejected his confession, but I did find out something you may find interesting."

I nod at her to continue, and she finally takes a seat across from me, tracing a green puzzle piece in her fingers. "Marcus said Knightley might suffer in the election because he isn't Southern Baptist or in a committed relationship."

That gets my full attention. "He... what? Why?"

"Sounded like the other two candidates are married with kids, and in the mindset of many, that means they can manage the town better. Plus Jay has the endorsement of the new president of the local Southern Baptist Association."

Disdain for small towns and denominational rivalries boils beneath the surface of my skin. "But he has *mayored,* or whatever word you would use, Juniper Grove just fine for his past term. He was elected by a landslide in the first round."

"He ran practically unopposed," she reminds me. "Of course it was a landslide victory. Times have changed these past four years. National politics are trickling down to local politics. Many people love Independent Darcy Marshall as our president because he's a centrist in this divided country. We know the democrat candidate doesn't stand a chance in this mayoral election, so many will vote for Jay since he's more of a centrist—while still being conservative—than Knightley is. And those who typically vote Republican will choose the Southern Baptist candidate over Knightley."

I stare at her, watching as she drops the puzzle piece and fidgets with her curly ponytail as if she didn't just speak "political reporter" fluently. "You should go into politics."

She barks out a laugh, shaking her head profusely. "Not a chance."

"A career in reporting on politics, then?"

"Nope. I only got the information I did from Marcus. He's the one who should dip his toes into that field. Not me."

Hm. *Interesting...*

"I guess I have to match Knightley with someone so that he can win this election. It's not like he's going to change his church denomination, nor would I want him to."

I smile brightly at Henrietta as she looks at me with horror, and then she clasps both hands over her mouth as if telling me all that was a secret. As I assemble the puzzle again, my brain spinning with date ideas for Knightley, Henrietta says she needs to go.

"Don't forget about the date with Reverend Philip next weekend! I'll text you both the details. After date three, you two should be good to go on your own." I beam with pride as I slide another piece into place. She shouts something unintelligible as she exits my room.

This is it. The golden ticket I need to launch my matchmaking business full-scale. If I am successful with Knightley, the hot, young mayor of Juniper Grove who has been single for the past eight years since his wife died in a tragic accident on their honeymoon, then I can make this business work for me.

Guilt tugs at my consciousness, warning me that I shouldn't celebrate this, especially since Cami, his former wife, basically became a part of our family when she started dating Knightley. Her death sent shockwaves through her hometown of Willow Bay and here; she was once the sweetheart of her town, much like Hartfield chose me for whatever reason. We had a lot of things in common apart from our platinum-blonde hair. As I've gotten older, I've come to understand just how much common ground we shared.

Both of our mothers died giving birth to us. We both were raised by a rich, doting father. We both were homeschooled, taught to speak French and Spanish, and both loved Knightley Austen. Well, she loved him romantically, and I loved him as an older brother at my mere age of eleven when they married.

One thing that sets our personalities apart, however, was when she was seventeen—I was seven years old—she disappeared for three months from her hometown. The local news and investigators speculated about it, and I was intrigued by the case. Nothing ever came to light, though. She was gone, and then she was back. It was after that she moved and met Knightley in college at Ole Miss. She stayed here with us while on college breaks. To this day, I don't know what happened to her, but whenever I wanted to play dolls with her, a hollow look would flash across her face, and she'd mindlessly reach behind her neck. She always wore turtlenecks. Even in the heat of a Mississippi summer. Even when she'd take us down to the coast to vacation in Willow Bay for a few days out of each summer.

I miss her often, and my heart aches for Knightley because I know he must miss her much more than I do.

I shake my head, detouring from walking further down memory lane.

Cami would want this for me. She'd want Knightley to find love again, and she'd want me to be successful. That is something I know for sure. She loved me and treated me like a little sister. More so than my actual older sister who rarely returns home from London to visit.

The biggest hurdle I face is that I've heard Knightley tell Papa he's sworn off marriage. Papa was thrilled as he knows the pain of losing a spouse is unbearable. He didn't want to see Knightley possibly go through that pain twice. Which is why Papa himself has never sought to remarry. Mama was it for him, and while I never knew her, I know by the way he talks of her that I remind him the most of her.

That's why I'll remain single. That and I can't give a man children. Most likely, but to me, the slightest inclination that I can't is enough to say that it won't happen.

But Knightley is still young at thirty-six. He's got a lot of life ahead of him, and he would make some woman very happy, no doubt. He could have kids with her.

He could make you happy, a mousy voice in my head squeaks. Pft, as if. I swat the ignorant thought away as if it's a gnat buzzing around my face. Nonsensical thoughts from his lousy, stupid, unintentional flirting.

The man is thirteen years older than me. He's basically family. He reminded me of that yesterday as he ruffled my head like I was an inconsequential child. No matter that he held me tightly throughout the film. No matter that he smelled like spruce and vanilla and buttery popcorn with a hint of chocolate. No matter how my insides turned to mush somewhere near the halfway point of the movie because being in his arms made me feel warm and safe.

Knightley George Austen is off limits, and even if he were on limits, he'd never go for the younger, off-brand version of his first wife. Cami was gentle, kind, and wrapped everyone around her finger by being genuinely good. I have to trick people into thinking I'm someone worthy of love and affection. I have to make everyone think I'm perfect, because if they find out I'm not, I'm—

A knock at the door startles me, and I realize I've broken the pen that was on my table. When did I even pick it up?

Black ink coats my hands, trickling onto my beloved puzzle pieces, as Papa announces his presence.

"Emma Jane, for supper, do you…" His question hangs in the air as he notices my ink-stained hand. "What happened, darling? Are you okay?"

He's at my side in seconds, moving quicker than I've seen him do in a while. "Oh, you're crying. Honey, what's wrong?"

Papa pushes hair out of my face, and I quickly drag my clean hand up to my cheeks. Yep, sure enough. They are damp. When did I start crying? And a better question… why?

"I'm fine. Was just thinking of how unfortunate it is that Henrietta may soon become a bride."

Papa sways. He places both hands on my puzzle table, knocking a few pieces to the ground as he does. "Oh, dear. Not another one. Did someone put something into the Hartfield water tower? Emma Jane, are you sure you should be matchmaking? You are too perceptive to love for your own good. Eventually, you'll match yourself…"

"Papa." I stand and hug him from behind, careful not to get ink on his nice, tan sweater. He swears there are many drafts in this house and dresses accordingly even though it's a humid hell outside. "I'm not going anywhere. You know that. Marriage was never in the cards for me. I think God saw to that." I've never told Papa about my PCOS diagnosis. He is too sickly himself. I don't need him fretting over me.

He turns and embraces me. "You shouldn't get married because it can rip your golden heart out, Emma Jane. That doesn't mean you are not someone worthy of marriage. I hope you know that."

I feel the tear as it slides down my cheek this time. "Thank you, Papa. But still. I'm yours forever, okay?"

He kisses the top of my head, and I'm reminded of Knightley's actions from last night. Fatherly affection. Is that what he was trying to get across when he messed with my hair? It's something my father would do.

I sigh. Why does it matter? I'm going to set him up with the most perfect woman I can find in the area. If I have a say in it, he will not lose this election simply because of old religious-based mindsets that a man can only run a town if he can run a family or is Southern Baptist.

Did no one ever read where Paul said it was better not to marry? That being unmarried means you can devote more time to the Lord?

Isn't that a good thing?

"Oh, Jane invited us over for supper. Do you want to go?"

My stomach knots. "Will Knightley be present?"

"No. He's working late at his law firm."

I breathe a sigh of relief, but also... I feel disappointed. "Then yes. Let's meet Jane for supper."

KNIGHTLEY

If one more person at this church tells me they wish they could move to Juniper Grove to vote for me, I might lose my mind.

Or at the very least, I may find a church closer to my house in Juniper Grove instead of driving out here every Sunday.

No, I wouldn't do that. This place, these people—though nosy and intrusive—are truly my home.

"Oh, Knightley, dear." Ms. Mary Bates tugs my arm as I'm trying to exit the small white building that's currently my nemesis. "I heard you have new competition. If I could move to Juniper Grove..."

"Thank you, Ms. Bates. Your vocal support of my political endeavors means a great deal to me." A great deal of poop, but she doesn't need to know that.

Thankfully, Henrietta catches her attention and drags her away from me with a knowing smile. One can always count on Henrietta to corral Ms. Bates. Ms. Bates is Henrietta's aunt. She adopted

Henrietta after her parents were killed in a plane crash. I mouth the words *thank you* and then make my escape.

I notice Emma Jane talking with the reverend, and I have half the mind to go over there simply because I don't like the way he's looking at her. I'm beginning to wonder if this man is fit to lead a church, but not because he is single. It's more about the way he leers at Emma Jane and his lousy personality that he tries to hide. Marcus told me about running into Henrietta after her date with the reverend, and I'm highly perturbed at the way the man acted.

Opting to mind my own business for now, I walk across the lawn to the parking lot and get into my car.

I travel the short distance from Hartfield Presbyterian Church to Henry's house for our traditional Sunday lunch. The antebellum house is a sight to behold with its classic Georgian style. I always thought I'd like to live here one day amidst the deep green grasses and old civil war bunker turned into a shed out in the back. With Bella, Emma Jane's sister, living in London, the only person the house will be left to is Emma Jane.

Or me.

But Emma Jane doesn't need to know that I promised her father I'd take over the estate if Emma Jane ran off and got married.

No one else has made it here yet, but I walk inside anyway because Henry gave me a key eons ago. I hang my dress coat on the golden rack by the door and walk through the entryway until I arrive at the sitting room. Henry gives the housekeepers Friday through Sunday off, so I gather logs from the rack tucked away in the corner of the room and get the fire started. Maybe Henry won't complain about random drafts if the fire is already hot and going.

The rest of us are sure to begin sweating, but it's his house, and we all care about the sensitive man greatly.

Before long, Henry and Emma Jane arrive, followed by my mom, who is on the phone with my brother, John. Henry takes a seat near the fire and closes his eyes while Mom and Emma Jane head toward the kitchen. Henry must be having an off day, so I lay a thin blanket over him and join the women to help prep our meal.

"Knightley, be a dear and grab the boiled eggs from the fridge. E. J. said they should be inside a blue container." I look around for the short, platinum blonde firecracker, but she's nowhere to be seen. After grabbing the eggs, I watch my mom, whose silver hair is fixed into a neat bun as she moves around the kitchen like she owns the place. This was our family's second home after Dad passed away. When Henry's wife died, he and Mom found companionship in one another. It's never been romantic, but the two have a deep friendship like I've never seen. Something deeper than what I have with Emma Jane or what I had with Cami before she passed away. An understanding only grief can create.

The thought of Cami stuns me for a second as it always does when she pops up in my head without warning. And right as I'm staring into the past, as well as presently at the kitchen entrance where Mom just disappeared through, Emma Jane comes into view wearing a pretty pink sundress, her shoulder-length hair framing her face perfectly.

My gut clenches and my head spins.

Emma Jane looks stunning, and the guilt I feel over that thought while thinking of my deceased wife leaves me breathless.

I shake my head then come to my senses as Emma Jane checks me as if I've lost it. "You okay?"

"There was a… bug," I say, swatting at perfectly clear air. Maybe I have lost it. I'd be lying if I said I hadn't noticed Emma Jane's *womanness* over the past couple of years. But noticing it while having a moment of missing Cami… it feels wrong.

Which leads me to a ridiculous comparison of the two that I can't help but make. Emma Jane is snarky and full of fight, whereas Cami was always the sweet and go-with-the-flow type, even when she challenged me. Emma Jane demands to be the center of attention, whereas Cami would shy away from it. I remember countless conversations where she would cry in my arms over feeling like she couldn't step out of line even once because her town expected perfection from her.

Though they shared platinum blonde hair and tan skin, Cami was tall and slim whereas Emma Jane is short and curvy. Cami had sharp features whereas Emma Jane's face is softer, her eyes more of an almond shape. Her lips are fuller. Pouty.

Something hits my forehead, and I rip my attention from her mouth. Emma Jane's eyebrows are knitted together, and she holds a rag, which I'm assuming is what snapped against my forehead. "Why are you looking at my lips? Stop being weird."

Heat crawls up my neck, deepening when I catch Mom across the kitchen island, sneaking glances our way while wearing a satisfied smile.

"You wish I was," I mumble unintelligibly.

She quips back. "In your dreams, Squire."

It's on the tip of my tongue to retort with "maybe tonight," but I smack my lips together to hold it in. That's crossing a line. A line I accidently pole vaulted over two nights ago when I invited her over to watch a movie with me.

I couldn't tell you what came over me, and I surmise it's the simple fact that I've begun to *notice* Emma Jane, and it's been a long time since I've dated or even thought of a woman.

Emma Jane laughs. "See? You're already wetting your lips thinking about it." Then she casually calls over her shoulder. "Jane, come get your son. He's hitting on me again."

Mom shocks me when she says, "It's about time he's sticks his toe over the friendship line."

We both tear our attention from each other and redirect to Mom. I screech, "I am not," just as Emma Jane says breathlessly, "He is not."

I motion toward her as if she alone verified the authenticity of my statement.

"Again?" Jane asks. "When did he hit on you the first time?"

My face flames with heat, and I cut my eyes to Emma Jane. Is she going to tell my mother that I told Emma Jane I wanted her to *need* me? *Oh, heavens... please no. Don't do it, Janie. Don't—*

Emma Jane swallows, shifting her reddened face from me to my mother, and then she blurts, "I'm actually going to matchmake Knightley. I was simply testing out his flirting game."

Thank you, Lord.

Wait, what?

At this statement, Mom exits the kitchen once more, and I stalk the short distance until I'm hovering over Emma Jane. "No. You are not meddling in my love life."

She throws a saucy smile up at me. "Of course not. Your love life doesn't exist. I'm helping you create one."

I try to think of a smart remark, but... she's right. Still not happening, though. "I don't need a love life."

"Everyone needs a love life." She clicks her tongue.

"Then set yourself up. Last I heard you're single. And you've never been on a date. How can you even match people when you've never experienced love?"

Hurt flashes across her blue eyes, and I immediately regret my words. But she's already talking before I can apologize.

"I know love. I love Papa, and he loves me. I love my sister, and she loves me. I love Henrietta, and she loves me. I love yo—" She stops herself mid-sentence, the hurt replaced with something like horror mixed with disbelief. She shifts her gray-blue eyes away from me before continuing. "I love you. As a friend. I know friendship and familial love. The only thing that would make romantic love different from what I know is the physical stuff. And we can get along just fine without it."

I scoff, running my hand through my hair. How can she so easily dismiss romantic love? Especially when she's trying to match people for a living! I lean down, captivating her full attention, then speak slowly. "Romantic love is so much more than friendship. It's more than being family. It's a committed lifetime. It's knowing someone at their darkest and loving them anyway. It's needing their touch to bring relief to your anxiety. It's drowning in their kiss when you've had an awful, hard day. It's laying your head next to someone each and every night, knowing they have the power to destroy you but trusting that they love you and will choose to enliven you."

Emma Jane never breaks contact, and we are close enough I smell the butterscotch on her breath from her church candies. The urge to close my eyes and minimize the remaining distance between us surprises me, and I fling myself backward, stumbling over my own feet. Emma Jane reaches out for me, and as my hand closes around hers, I realize that she's not preventing me from falling.

She's coming down with me.

As I crash toward the tiled floor, I hold Emma Jane close against me to prevent her from hitting the ground. She lands on my chest as my back slams against the dark blue marble floor, knocking the breath from my lungs. We are a mess of entwined limbs and pained groans. When her eyes lock with mine, I feel a surge of heat course through my veins. Her hair creates a wall against the outside world, and I think I might want to kiss her within this private nook on the floor.

It's been eight years since I've kissed a woman...

"Emma Jane. Do you mind?" I wish I could say my words sound annoyed, but they sound like a desperate plea. *Emma Jane. Do you mind getting off of me? Because I'm about to snap and kiss you. And I really shouldn't do that because you're* you.

"Oh, right. Um..." She frantically scrambles to get off me, but because of the way we are tangled together, she only manages to straddle me before she falls over, her hands bracing against my chest as her molten gaze suggests she might want to kiss me, too. *Oh, God… Give me strength…*

It's not that I want Emma Jane particularly, I tell myself. It's that I've been starved of this type of affection for a long while. I forgot how good it felt to desire a woman.

"What is going on here?" Henry's booming voice looms over us, and that is enough to get Emma Jane back solidly on her feet. I grunt as I get up, my body reminding me that no matter how much I run and work out, I'm thirty-six.

And she's twenty-three.

I grunt again, but this time because I'm disgusted with myself. I'm not allowed to have thoughts about Emma Jane because she's her. She's like a little sister.

But she's not, my brain helpfully reminds me.

She's too young for me. Thirteen years is a ginormous gap, especially when she's in her *early* twenties…

It's not like you just met her. You've known her forever.

Precisely! She's the textbook definition of off-limits, I battle with my thoughts.

"Knightley was being his clumsy self and started to fall, but when I tried to help, he brought me down with him." Emma Jane laughs nervously as if she was caught in a precarious situation.

It feels like we were caught doing *something* judging by the way Henry is glaring at me.

Emma Jane elbows me, and I cackle a little too loudly alongside her. "Yep. That's what happened." And it *is* what happened, so why does it feel like I'm lying?

"Knightley isn't clumsy." Henry's monotone voice sends chills down my spine.

Mom lingers with a knowing look at the doorway of the kitchen as Henry leaves. We all set to work continuing to prepare lunch. Emma Jane approaches the topic of matchmaking me with someone again, and of course, I shoot her down.

Again and again and again I shoot her down, even when she tries to convince me she will find a "lovely woman."

It's not that I'm opposed to love. I'm opposed to falling in love again only to have said love ripped from my fingers. Better to not risk that possibility. I've come to terms with the accident and have gotten over being angry at God for it all, but that doesn't mean I want to go through that again, even if it means experiencing romantic love once more.

Even if it means finding someone who makes me *feel things* again...

Which is the icing on the cake as to why whatever just happened between me and Emma Jane—and whatever nonsense got into me the other day in my home when I flirted with her and got dizzy on her scent while she hid herself away in my arms throughout the movie—is irrelevant. Dead. A moot point, as we say in law when something up for discussion is of no importance.

However, after we all sit down at the long dining table to eat our meal, Emma Jane shows me a picture of a pretty brunette with a charming smile and kind eyes. Emma Jane says her name is Mallory and that I'm supposed to meet her at seven p.m. sharp on Friday night. Emma Jane argues that if all goes well, then having a girlfriend could boost my poll numbers. It's the most idiotic of ideas, but...

For some reason...

I quit fighting her on it.

Maybe if I date another woman then I'll stop having completely inappropriate thoughts and impulses toward Emma Jane.

It'll be my first date since I took the stunning blonde from college out for ice cream after exams. After that first one I knew I never wanted to go on a first date again.

But God had other plans.

Emma Jane

Rule #7: Celebrate with your clients when they become official!

Lucy Spence walks into Books and Beans, and on her heels follows her boss, Stone Harper.

But is he…?

My eyes bulge out of my head as I watch the tall, handsome, and brawny man with a chiseled jaw and honey blond hair wrap his arm around her waist, spin her into his side, and kiss her square on the lips.

The initial shock of the picture before me wears off, replaced with a buzzing excitement for my older friend from college.

The girl finally did it.

She snagged her hot boss.

The mug I'm drying off fumbles in my hand, but I steady it and set it on the counter, a wide grin stretching across my face. "Hi, Lucy." I look over her shoulder to the man who constantly reminds me to keep Lucy's romance book stocked. No wonder…

Lucy fingers her strawberry bangs, which match the color of her face right now. She's wearing high-waisted skinny jeans with a blue tank top tucked in and white sneakers.

And I point this out because Stone mirrors her in his light wash jeans, blue t-shirt, and white sneakers.

I want to throw confetti at the two of them for finally becoming official, but then I'd have to clean it up, and I'm not in the market to create extra work for myself later today. It'll prevent me from putting the polishing touches on my new website: Emma Jane's Guide to Matchmaking.

And when I post Knightley's success, I'll add to his column: the Mayor.

"Emma Jane?" Lucy says, scrunching her nose and narrowing her eyes in evaluation. Probably of my sanity since I know I just left earth there for a second.

"Sorry, I've got news to share with you." Now it's my turn to examine her. "But it seems you do, too."

Stone responds, "She finally agreed to date me." The way he looks down at her, like she hung the moon and stars, simultaneously makes joy and longing swell within me.

I allow the joy to take over and shove the longing deep, deep down.

"I'm so happy for you two! Both of your coffees are on me today, okay?"

"For getting into a relationship?" Stone muses. "Guess I need to do that more often."

Lucy elbows him and gives him a smile I can only describe as both loving and deadly. "We need the coffee to go today, E. J."

The man has been in this coffee shop with many different women since I've been employed here, but I noticed that stopped a few months ago. I wonder if it was because of Lucy.

I shrug, already starting on both of their usual orders. "I love love. It should be celebrated. If the two of you didn't come together organically, you were definitely on my list to matchmake for my new business."

Lucy and Stone eye each other like they are sharing a secret no one else is privy to. Guess that's what coupling up does to people. Finally, she turns to me. "Oh, did you finally get your website up?"

"Want to see it?"

"Of course I do!" She breaks free from Stone and does what only a few people ever get to do: she comes around to my side of the coffee bar. I set to work pulling up the mobile design of my website, showing her all the features from my compatibility checklists, the service inquiry form, the testimonial section (where only Halle and Grant reside currently), and the free guide on how to matchmake in case anyone can't afford my services and wants to try to get the love of their lives for themselves.

"This is amazing, E. J. I'm so glad you've found what you want to do." She gets this faraway look in her eyes that sometimes happens when she's got a story idea. "I think I want to write a romantic comedy about a matchmaker now!"

I laugh and set my phone down. "I'll be your resource. I haven't been studying the topic of romantic love for long, but I've studied psychology and sociology throughout my time homeschooling and in college as part of my business major."

"I got the romance part down. In fact, I could help you with some tweaks on your compatibility form if you'd like." Lucy walks back to Stone, who has been leaning against the counter and scrolling on his phone. When she rejoins him, he puts his phone away and kisses her on the cheek. That twinge of desire reignites, and I douse it once more with water.

"Great! Let's meet up later in the week." I finish making their coffee, give it to them, and they leave. For the rest of the shift, I contemplate if now is the time to quit this job. I started working here because it got me out of the house. Papa has always been great at giving me money to budget for myself every month, but it can be suffocating alone in that large home with only him and ghosts of my mother in every picture frame I pass.

"Bye, Kelsey." I wave to my younger coworker before leaving. As I'm stepping through the door and planning to go grocery shopping, an ache spreads across my lower abdomen, rerouting my plans for the rest of the day the same way the disease reroutes mature eggs during ovulation. I have missed my last two periods, so this day was bound to happen.

Trying not to double over at the ever increasing pain, I make it to my car and speed through town to try and make it the twenty minutes home to Hartfield.

My skin rips from my upper lip, leaving a burning, red mustache.

Okay, it's just a mark from the wax strip, but still.

It's better than the hair that was previously darkening in the area. PCOS: a gift that keeps on giving. Hairy edition.

I called out of my morning shift today because after I got home yesterday, things only went downhill.

Flowed downhill.

Like an angry mudslide.

My stomach churns again, and I reposition myself from my vanity mirror in the bathroom to the actual toilet.

Papa has come up to check on me twice, but he only thinks I have a stomachache. Not to mention it's left him breathless to walk the stairs both times he's done it today. I told him to stay away because I don't want him catching my sickness.

Which will never happen, but still. I don't want him wearing himself out over something completely out of his control. I've managed this on my own—well, Halle helped me for a while there—since I was fifteen. I know what I'm doing now at twenty-three.

So anyways, to say I'm startled when a knock on my door sounds is an understatement.

"Emma Jane? Are you decent?"

And this day just got unbelievably worse.

"Not right now," I holler through my cracked-open bathroom door hoping he can hear me from outside of my bedroom. I scramble to finish my business, not bothering to check myself in the mirror before quickly washing my hands and tucking myself into bed while still wearing yesterday's pajama set.

"Emma?" He one-named me, which means he's about to burst in this room without my consent.

"Hold on, Squire." I situate myself upright in bed with my legs tucked to my chest to try and relieve the pain. Crying to myself and folding into the fetal position isn't an option at the moment, though it was my chosen pose for most of the morning. "Come in."

Knightley doesn't hesitate, and he's armed with...

A tray of food?

I can't contain my laugh at the image of Knightley standing in my doorway like he's my personal servant. I don't have one of those, but if I did, I'd want him to be a complete replica of the man standing across my room.

Knightley is objectively hot, and any woman in her right mind would want to gaze upon that perfect image all day. He's wearing dark maroon plaid pants with a solid black button down tucked in. His black socks are barely visible and his rusty brown dress shoes are polished.

He came from his law firm.

"I brought soup and electrolytes. Henry said you had a stomach virus and wanted someone to check in on you."

"He could have sent one of the housekeepers."

Knightley shrugs, which causes the liquids on the tray to slosh over the edges of their containers. He straightens and, with careful steps, walks to my bedside. He smells like a breath of fresh air, a nice change to the stagnant air of this room I haven't left except for a couple of times to go down to the kitchen.

I adjust, attempting to straighten my legs so he can set the tray on top of them, but the angry wasps in my stomach sting in rebellion. I can't hold in the moan that arises in my throat.

Knightley sets the wooden tray on the nightstand, knocking my chapstick, speaker, and current matchmaking book onto the floor. He sits down on the edge of the bed, worry shining in his pretty blue eyes. "Are you okay? Do I need to get something for you to throw up in?"

I shake my head, and he visibly relaxes. But then as he looks me over in my balled up position, his jaw loosens, and he lets out a little "oh" sound.

"You're not sick, it's just your..." He lets the word period hang in the air.

I nod, not even feeling embarrassed. It's so much more than just my period, but he doesn't need to know that.

He looks at the tray then back to me, concern etched across his sharp features. "You should still eat the soup and drink the electrolyte water. It's good for you." His eyes flick to my lips, and I feel it down to my toes. Or maybe I just need to go to the bathroom again. "Do you, uh, need anything else?"

My stomach gurgles, and I'm sure of it. "Nope. I'm a big girl. I can take care of myself." I move around in bed until I'm shoving at him to get up. He doesn't hesitate. "Now leave."

Knightley does as I ask. When he shuts my door, I throw the blankets off me and hop out of bed, but dizziness sweeps over me,

and I fall toward the floor, hitting the edge of the tray on the way
down as I fight to catch myself.

As the thankfully lukewarm soup and water cover me, Knightley
swings my door open, pauses, then he rushes over to me, falling to
his knees and moving the dishes off of me.

"You're not handling yourself well, Emma." His tone isn't condescending or mean. It's full of concern and fretfulness. "What's
going on? I've seen women on their cycles who function just fine.
You aren't functioning."

I brush noodles from my chest as he pulls them from my hair.
"It's different for every woman. I get dizzy sometimes. That's all.
Low iron and sugars and such."

"So dizzy that you collapse?"

"I got out of bed too fast. That's all. Speaking of, I need to go to
the bathroom."

He stands and offers his assistance. After he lifts me up, I attempt to take my hand back, but he doesn't let go. In fact, he's
squeezing a little too tightly. I glance from his death grip to his
face, prepared to make some comment about how he must revel
in holding my hand. But his eyes are nowhere near mine.

That's when I remember I'm in my pajamas.

A little pink matching tank top and shorts set.

Made of silk and lace.

Because it made me feel good when I felt so terrible.

I continue to watch him gape at me, and I don't think he realizes
what he's doing.

And why does his unbridled attention cause a sudden heat flash?

No, not him.

Must be the PCOS flare.

I yank my hand away, which causes me to stumble backwards just from the force. He snaps to attention, grabbing my arm.

"I wasn't falling." I place my hand on top of his, ignoring the pooling warmth in my stomach. The next words slip unbidden from my lips in an awfully coquettish tone. "At least not yet."

No ma'am. No playing flirty games with your older male friend today. Not dressed like *this*.

Knightley coughs, but doesn't let go of me. He looks at my lips again, and I'm left wondering if *he's* okay.

"I need to go to the bathroom," I reiterate.

In all seriousness, he says, "Let me walk you there."

"I'm fine, Knightley. I promise. Please just leave. Thank you for helping me. I'll get this cleaned later." I force myself to make my voice soft and gentle so he knows I'm all good.

"I'm going downstairs to talk to Henry and to send someone up to clean this. I'll be back in thirty minutes to check on you." And with that, he spins on his heel and walks back out my door. I rush to the bathroom and take care of my business. When I come out, it's like the mess was never created.

And my bed sheets are new.

With a bag of strawberry Lindor chocolates sitting on my pillow.

I can't help but smile. I change out of my clothes, opting for sweatpants and a tank top. Since my stomach is feeling better momentarily, I sit at my vanity and grab my brush. When I look in the mirror, a light gasp of horror escapes my lips.

I've been sporting that stupid red mustache from my waxing this entire time.

No wonder he kept looking at my lips.

KNIGHTLEY

E mma Jane Williams is a myriad of things.

She is selfish.

Calculating.

In her own head.

Admittedly brilliant.

Charming.

And most surprisingly…

Emma Jane is right about this woman.

Mallory Granger is, in fact, a lovely date.

The light-complected, brown-eyed brunette is currently scooping an expertly twirled forkful of linguini into her mouth, sighing with delight. "I'm so glad you chose this place."

Yeah, there's the issue. She thinks I chose the place, time, and day. That was all Emma Jane. Mallory knows this date is a "beta trial" of Emma Jane's matchmaking services, but she thinks the effort was mine.

And do I feel a smidge guilty over that?

Yes.

But also... I'm starting to think maybe this whole blind date wasn't such a bad idea after all.

"Do I have something on my face?" Mallory makes a motion to wipe the corners of her lips.

"No." I laugh.

She grins a bright white smile. "Good. But you do..."

Mallory leans across the narrow table, her fingers outstretched toward my face. Rapid thoughts race across my mind, the primary one being that I haven't so much as touched another woman romantically, much less been touched by one with uncertain romantic intentions.

Confusion flashes across her face when I lean back, followed by a gentle smile. She points to a spot on the corner of her mouth, and I take a napkin to mine. She gives me a thumbs up then starts to twirl more pasta. "Not a fan of physical contact?"

I shake my head. I love it, in fact. "I don't know if Emma Jane told you or not, but I'm widowed, and I haven't dated in eight years." I laugh hesitantly. "I'm out of practice."

She nods with understanding and apologizes for my loss. "She didn't tell me, but that makes sense."

"What do you mean by that?"

Mallory motions around the table and then between us. "You know, your awkwardness. You're the mayor of this town, and I've seen you stand in front of crowds and give speeches time after time.

Charisma comes naturally for you, but tonight it's like you have a mental checklist you're keeping track of. Kind of like—"

"Like I'm making sure I do all of the 'supposed tos' of dating," I finish for her with a relieved sigh. Last night, Emma Jane drilled me on proper date mannerisms. I halfway listened because at the time, I thought this date was only a show to get Emma Jane off my back, but from the moment I met Mallory outside, I instantly felt like I wanted to try.

She is attractive, yes, but something about her puts me at ease and feels more friendly. She's confident, collected, poised, and smart. Her quiet but witty demeanor reminds me of my ex-wife but in a different body.

And it doesn't upset me.

"I promise you, you're hitting all the 'supposed tos' very well." She takes a sip of red wine. "Just be yourself. This is only dinner with another human."

"You're right," I agree and sip the cool, tangy drink. "What about you? I'm curious as to why you're single."

"Never ask a woman that." She wiggles her finger back and forth in front of her face. "That is an instant turn-off."

"Why's that?" I ask, confused. Shouldn't it be a compliment that I think she has the personality and aura to have someone devoted to to her?

"Because it's received as a character flaw. Like there must be something wrong with me because I don't have a ring on my finger." Mallory speaks with ease and gentleness, not an ounce of condemnation or anger over the misinterpreted question.

But I can't contain the laughter that flows from me at how completely different our thought processes are. "Mallory, I'm going to be completely honest. I meant that question as a compliment. I don't think there is anything wrong with you based on what I've learned so far."

"I know." She grins, then shovels another forkful of food into her mouth. After she finishes chewing, she says with downcast eyes, "I'm widowed, too, you know? My husband passed away two years ago in a car accident."

In that instant, when we make eye contact, it's like a mutual understanding has been forged. I think of my mom and Henry. This is what it must be like for them. "An understanding only grief can create," I reiterate my thoughts from earlier this week. She nods and smiles, shoving more pasta into her mouth.

"Do you want to talk about him?"

"Maybe one day," she responds. "But I don't think that's a first-date conversation to be had. Why don't we talk about how handsome you are or how pretty I am and how cute our babies could be?" The lilt in her voice and crinkles around her eyes tell me she's joking. *I hope she is...*

"I like your confidence and..." I try to find the right word, "bravado. It's not over the top, and I find you quite fascinating."

"You're quite the charmer yourself, Mr. Knightley."

"So, you grew up in Washington, D. C., moved to Juniper Grove a year ago to work on the president's campaign, and you stuck around."

After Mallory dabs her lips with a napkin, she says, "I liked the slowness of life here. D. C. can feel like you're living at turbo speed. Living here feels like third gear at max."

I nod. "I've spent some time in D. C., and I couldn't imagine living there. I got into politics here because we didn't have any great candidates, and I saw improvements that needed to happen in this town. I don't think I'd ever pursue anything more. In fact, I think this will be my last term if I win reelection."

"Maybe I can run for office after you, then." She winks.

"You'll have to beat the independent candidate, Jay. Jansen Johnson. He's a formidable opponent. To be honest, I wouldn't be upset at all if he won. Yeah, it'd hurt my pride if the people of Juniper Grove didn't want me for a second term, but he's a good guy and has done a lot for this town."

I take a bite of my carbonara, wondering why in the world I'm telling her all of this. She's so easy to talk to; I'm spilling all my secrets.

"Sounds like you're just the man for the job. The best politicians are the ones who don't necessarily want to be politicians."

I shrug. "Maybe so. Oh, and if you want to win, you might need to become male and get married and join the Southern Baptist denomination." It started as poking fun, but by the end of my statement, even I admit I sound a little bitter.

"Well, I am a part of the Southern Baptist denomination, and I am open to marriage, obviously. But I don't think changing my gender is in the cards for me. I'm happily female, just as the Good Lord intended, and will continue living that way." She laughs. "Do you have something against my denomination?"

I squirm a little in my seat. "It's nothing against the denomination. It's more so against the new president of the local association. He misinterprets scripture a lot and seems to have a thing against me being Presbyterian."

"How so? Forgive me, but I haven't been in the loop of evangelical happenings lately."

"No worries. I wish I wasn't. He is promoting Jay over me because he's Southern Baptist and has a family. Vance Green, the president, has said on numerous occasions that he believes First Timothy 3:12 applies to all men who proclaim to be Christians in positions of leadership, not just those who are deacons. He's subtly stating he doesn't believe me to be a true Christian, and that stings to hear, you know?"

Mallory nods and offers a soft smile of understanding. "I can see how that would be hurtful. For the record, I think he's completely wrong. The scripture is clear without his wacky interpretation."

"Glad you agree." There's a pause in conversation, both of us taking sips of our respective drinks.

We make eye contact, and I realize there is no zing. Mallory is full of understanding and empathy, but she lacks...

What does she lack?

"Do you think we might be too alike, Knightley?" Mallory asks as if she's hunting around inside my brain.

Pressing my lips into a line, I nod.

That's it. That's the issue.

We agree too much.

The absence of a challenge is a wet rag on the miniscule amount of attraction I had for Mallory.

Laughing at my idiocy, I fold my hands in front of me and evaluate Mallory once more. She is beautiful, no doubt. Fun. Smart. Agreeable.

But I think I like my women a little... less agreeable.

A feisty blonde takes center stage within my thoughts, and I swallow the budding lump in my throat.

"I like you a lot, Mallory, I do, but..."

She holds up two petite hands. "Say no more. There's no romantic spark. Just the kindling of a sweet friendship. To be honest, I thought I was ready to date, but I don't think I'm as ready as I thought I was."

Breath exits my body, an easy smile slides over my face, and we slip into political conversation. We continue chatting throughout the rest of our dinner, and though the conversation is stimulating and we have a lot in common, no spark ignites.

I search for it in her laugh, in her smirk, in her body...

But nothing.

No "I have to kiss you right now" chemistry.

No challenge to be met.

When I hug her goodnight beside her car, there are no feelings of wanting to do it again or to not let go.

Not like when Emma Jane was in my arms or on top of me—

A knock at my driver's window thankfully pulls me from my inappropriate memories that need to be exorcized from my brain.

Which is not a word I need to think of, especially if I want to keep thoughts of Cami and her awful past at bay...

She never would tell me what happened during her time away, before she moved to north Mississippi, but I knew the pentagram branded into the back of her neck was nothing good. Couldn't be removed. We tried. The best we could do was tattoo colorful wildflowers over the nefarious brand, but even then, she refused to wear anything that revealed her neck while she was in public.

A shiver runs down my spine.

"What's up?" I ask Mallory. She points to her car.

"It won't start. My engine light is on. Do you think you could give me a lift home?"

"Of course," I say, right as a call from Marcus comes through. I answer as she gets into my truck, and he asks me to come over to talk about something he's conflicted about. I agree, but I want to change vehicles if I'm going to go out to Hartfield. "Where do you live?"

She tells me, and it's past my place. "Do you think we could stop at my house so I can switch vehicles? I'm going to visit a friend out in Hartfield after dropping you off."

"Not a problem, as long as you aren't trying to take me home..."

Heat crawls up my neck at the insinuation. "Uh, um, no. I'm not that kind of man."

"I know." She laughs, settling into the passenger seat. "I was just teasing. You're a great guy. I hope we get to work together politically one day. Let me know how I can help out with your campaign, okay? Oh! Actually, I have an idea if you're up for it."

I crank the truck. "What is it?"

"You're worried about losing because you're single, right?"

"Yes." I cut my eyes to her as I pull out of the restaurant's parking lot.

"Well, what if..."

We talk shop back and forth the short distance to my house. Her idea is bonkers, but honestly, it just might work. Politicians do this kind of stuff all the time, right?

Her offer is a rip current in my head, and you know what they say about rip currents: you have to swim with them. I turn into my gravel driveway, and my headlights reflect not just my car sitting in front of my house instead of in the garage where it should be, but also Emma Jane's car.

And Emma Jane.

Sitting on my steps with a wide grin directed at my truck.

I shut off the truck, which was blinding her.

Something inside me screams that I should stop Mallory from getting out of the truck, but that's crazy, right? This is what Emma Jane wanted...

She will be thrilled to hear our date went well even though we aren't romantically interested in each other. Mallory and I will have an image to keep up soon...

But the moment Mallory steps out of my truck, Emma Jane's eyes grow wide under the front porch light, and she shoots to her feet quicker than a bottle rocket going off on the Fourth of July.

Her smile falters for the briefest of seconds as she eyes Mallory, and when she turns in my direction, where I'm finally moving myself out of the truck on wobbling legs at the false implication of this moment, I swear I see her bare her teeth.

Emma Jane

I felt the way my smile twisted to a snarl.

My composed façade faltered for only a moment before I remembered I should be happy about this.

Granted, I didn't take Knightley to be the kind of man that takes a woman back to his place on the first date, but I guess you never truly know someone.

Even if they've been by your side since you've existed on this earth.

The unanswerable question remains: why am I not happy about this when it's what I wanted for him and my business? Why did I let my smile slip into a snarl? Why does this scene in front of me cut me like a serrated knife?

"Emma Jane, hey." His voice is higher than usual and panic is written across his face. "What are you doing here this late? Is everything okay with Henry?"

Nice going, dude. Use my father as the reason a woman is on your doorstep in the middle of the night when you're trying to bring another woman home.

I can do one of two things here.

I can continue to say something about my father to help him out, or…

"Nothing like that. Papa's fine. I left my favorite jacket over here the other day after our movie night. Thought I'd swing by to pick it up."

I'm not happy about the immature direction I chose to go, but one look in Mallory's direction tells me she couldn't care less.

She's amused. Her arms hang by her curves, which are showing nicely in a killer black dress (I want to ask her where she got it from), and the corner of her lip ticks up as if she's fighting a smile.

"Emma Jane Williams? It's nice to finally meet you!" Mallory steps in front of Knightley, who still hasn't gained his composure. His flustered state reminds me that I at least need to get my act together and not ruin this for him.

I reach out my hand, and she meets me halfway. "Yes! So sorry I'm imposing on your night. I had no idea he would be bringing you back here, and I was anxiously waiting to hear how the date went since you two are beta testing my program."

Mallory and Knightley exchange looks, and everything I need to know about the two of them cements in my brain.

And I don't know if I'm thrilled or disappointed.

Thrilled. Definitely over the moon excited that they just looked at each other in that secret couple-y way Stone and Lucy looked at each other in front of me.

Before I can change my mind and let this weird disappointment win out, I say, "I can see the two of you are doing just fine, so I'm going to go now. Enjoy the rest of your night."

I wave then walk to my car, careful not to move to the pace of my heart beating out of my chest. I take caution not to slam my door closed and not to drive aggressively out of the drive, but once I'm out of sight, for some unholy reason, I scream.

I yell, hit the steering wheel, and wonder why in the world I'm having such a visceral, untamed reaction to Knightley taking a woman home.

It's what I wanted!

Literally.

I matched them! I found her through social media and, after having a few pleasant conversations, determined she would be a fantastic fit for him.

Maybe it's just the shattered illusion of thinking Knightley was a decent man who fully committed to a woman before bringing her to bed.

But who knows if that's what he was doing, Emma Jane?

My brain is a battleground; which version of my Knightley will win out?

My.

In an instant, my anger melts away. My screams become hysterical laughs, and now, instead of beating the steering wheel, I rub it as if I'm apologizing for treating it as a punching bag.

"Wow, miss ma'am. No wonder you got upset." I laugh more to myself, a tear running down my cheek. *My Knightley.* Somewhere along the way of being shoved together often, I think he became one of my best friends. He became someone I trust and respect even if we go for each others' throats often.

As much as he has criticized me, he's never been wrong. That's a thought I'll have to sit with.

So, if he marries another woman, I'll lose my close friendship with him. He will no longer be mine. I'll have to let him go.

But I don't know if I'm ready for that.

With a relieved sigh at realizing the cause for my reaction was the idea of losing my friend instead of jealousy over Mallory and Knightley—though I still can't believe he took her home after the first date—I wipe the tears from my eyes and focus on making it back to Hartfield in one piece.

Once I'm home, I take a thirty-minute shower from hell, relishing in the hot water as it numbs the tension in my body. Any lingering thoughts of Knightley and Mallory swirl down the drain as I get out, do my nighttime skincare routine, and then climb into my comfortable bed.

As I lay in bed attempting to get comfortable, a text dings on my phone.

I have all notifications silenced at this time at night.

All except his.

Squire: It's not what you think. The date did go well, but not that well.

Bubbling laughter escapes through my lips. *Oh, thank God!* Not that it's any of my business, but I'm glad to know he isn't the kind of man to sleep with a woman on the first date.

Me: No judgment here. Glad it went well.

There was immense judgment on my end. Lots of it. But he doesn't need to know that.

He immediately begins typing.

Squire: Thank you for tonight.

Me: Are you broken? I was eighty-five percent worried you'd bail on the date, and now you're thanking me?

Squire: I thought about bailing. But I'm glad I didn't. It was… nice.

I type.

Delete.

Type again.

Delete.

With a heavy sigh and new tension built up in my shoulders, I place my phone on the charger and roll face-first into my pillow. He had a nice night with Mallory. That's wonderful. It's—as I've reminded myself a million times—what I wanted.

So why does it feel like someone is taking a puzzle piece from my life and refusing to give it back, leaving me incomplete for all eternity?

I awake from fitful sleep at four in the morning to tears running down my face and a Snapchat from Halle.

What is she doing up this early?

She sends a black screen, so I ask her if she wants to video call.

The dream comes back to me in full force, though to be honest, it never left. Knightley standing at the altar of Hartfield Presbyterian Church. Mallory walking down the aisle in a beautiful and expensive white gown that I'd kill for. The congregation applauding, Papa blubbering, and this time, instead of trying to lift his spirits, I'm blubbering right alongside Papa.

My phone rings, and moments later, Halle's tired face and messy blonde hair fills the screen.

"Have you been crying?" We both say that at the same time, which causes us both to laugh until the sound turns to cries.

After a stuffy sniffle, Halle says, "You go first."

"I set Knightley up on a date, and he—" I pause for a second, wondering if I should tell Halle. She knows him well, and I don't want her viewing him in an unfavorable light. But then again, Halle is my person, and she's always been there for me. "He took the woman home. I was waiting on his porch to ask him how the date went, and when he pulled up, she got out of his truck."

Halle is silent for a moment, on the soft sounds of her continual sniffling. "Tell me, Emma Jane, why does this bother you exactly?"

"Because I'm going to lose him. He's my friend, Halle."

"Why do you say you'll lose him?"

I think for a moment, tucking a strand of loose hair behind my ear, before answering. "Because we won't get to do game nights together, or watch movies together at his house, or just go on walks together. If he has a woman, then I can't be with him privately like that for the sake of boundaries. He won't tell me I'm moronic for pursuing a new business venture, and I won't get to sass him back and tell him he's wrong, only for me to prove him right down the line. I'm not a kid like I was when he married Cami. It's not the same now. If he commits to Mallory, then I have to step down." Something is definitely different. I've been denying that for a while, but things have shifted between us.

"While I am immensely proud of your insight and wisdom in this manner, I am so sorry you're hurting, E. J." Halle's brown eyes shine with sympathy. We sit in silence for a minute before she speaks again. "Are you upset that you will lose the closeness of your friendship? Or, be honest here, do you wish you were Mallory?"

"Oh, definitely the first." I wave my hand dismissively. "You know I'm never getting married. You know I can't do that to a man." She's the only one who knows, apart from my doctor and Henrietta. Halle has always been a mother figure to me; she's the one who took me to all the appointments to figure out why my periods weren't consistent. It all came to a head when I was fifteen and swore my appendix was rapturing.

No, it was giant cysts on my ovaries.

"Knightley isn't just any man, though. He's... Knightley."

"Exactly. He's Knightley. Thirteen years older than me. Widowed. The mayor of a whole town. I'm like his little sister." Except for when he flirts with me. Then I feel like I might be something more, but I shove that thought way down into the depths. It's harmless teasing, nothing more. Even if it feels new and exciting.

"You're twenty-three, know him better than any other woman out there besides maybe his own mother, are launching your own business, and are more mature than most women I know.

You've had to be, E. J." Her tone gives way to the usual you-lost-your-mom-as-a-baby-and-had-to-raise-yourself inflection. I never understood why people took that voice with me but never did with Henrietta. She lost both of her parents for heaven's sake. Yet, the town doesn't coddle her like they do me.

I can't help the laugh that bubbles out. *If only she could have seen me in the car last night...*

Yeah, reeeeal mature.

"Are you trying to get me to date Knightley? Because if so, I need you to redirect your thoughts. Let me do the matchmaking, Halle. You just enjoy your marital bliss."

She grins at me. "Someone has to look out for you while you look out for everyone else in your life. Be honest with yourself, Emma Jane."

I sigh, accidentally dropping the phone. I pick it back up and stare into her brown eyes, setting my jaw. "Fine. He's wonderfully challenging and smart and handsome, and I think I may be into him. But I can't do anything about it, Halle. I just matched him with a woman who can be everything I can't be for him."

"That is a predicament for you. Especially if he liked her. But what if he didn't?"

I scoff. "He took her home. Of course he liked her."

"You don't know why they went back to his place. It could be completely innocent."

"He said it was, but still. He took her to his place. What am I supposed to do? Tell him I like his stupid face? Tell him that over the past two years, I've slowly begun to see him in a different light until it slapped me across the face last night? Tell him that I love it when he fights with me and puts me in my place and brings me strawberry chocolates when I'm on my period? Tell him I love the way he protects other people and love the way he stays true to his faith through this campaign even though he's being attacked left and right?"

Halle can't seem to erase the smile off her face. "That's exactly what you do, Emma Jane. You lay your cards on the table."

I've never been the one to lay my cards down. I hold them tight to my chest, waiting for other players to make their moves before I show my hand. Life's a huge game, and I don't like to lose. But I don't cheat to win.

Redirecting this uncomfortable conversation, I ask, "Why were you crying?"

Her smile falters. "Well, E. J., I haven't told anyone yet, so let's keep this between me and you." She chews on her bottom lip, her eyes falling down to look at something outside of my frame. Then, she holds up a stick that kind of looks like a thermometer. "I'm pregnant."

Immediately, calculations begin inside my head as I spout out congratulations. "But you guys haven't even been married for a whole month." I blurt the words without even thinking of the implications.

Halle's cheek pinken. "Grant and I may have slipped up before our wedding night." She pegs me with a sharp gaze. "But you better not. Wait until you say the vows to each other and to God. It's hard to wait, but it's better to be obedient to the Lord."

"Not getting married," I remind her, then we both release tired laughs. "But I am very happy for the two of you, regardless of how the baby came to be."

"Thank you, Emma Jane. I'm excited, too, but I'll have to tell Grant in the morning, and I'm kind of nervous. I'm forty. This isn't normal. What if everything goes wrong?" She doesn't have to say *like with your mother.*

I reach toward the screen, wishing I could give her a huge hug. "But what if everything goes right?"

Halle smiles, and it meets her eyes. "You're right."

We chat for a little longer, pray over her pregnancy, and then hang up.

Huh. She couldn't wait until her wedding night? What does that feel like? Is sex that good?

I've only kissed a couple of guys, and well, let's just say they were chaste and never happened again. I stopped dating after the second one during my sophomore year in college. Dating felt pointless. I don't think I've ever had the desire to go further than those awful kisses.

Maybe it's the PCOS. Another reason I shouldn't get married—no sex drive.

I let out a frustrated groan into my pillow before sitting up in bed.

Why did Halle have to go there? Why did she have to make me realize I've been entertaining the idea of *more* with Knightley without even knowing it? It can never happen, so I have to bury these pesky feelings.

Knowing there is no way I am going to go back to sleep, I get up, run downstairs for coffee, and then return to my room to work on my current puzzle while I piece together my thoughts surrounding the unattainable Knightley George Austen.

I've never had a crush before.

Zero-out-of-ten recommend.

Emma Jane

RULE #10: THOROUGH RESEARCH IS REQUIRED. DON'T SKIP OUT ON OTHER POSSIBILITIES OUTSIDE OF YOUR OWN PREMONITIONS.

A branch violates me as I maneuver along the side of the seafood restaurant, tucking myself low in the decorative bushes outside the windows of the building that give way to a clear view of Henrietta and—

"What the—" I hiss. Marcus Long is sitting across from her in the spot that's reserved for Reverend Elton Philip. My nose touches the window, and I yank myself backward to keep from accidentally making out with the nasty glass. Henrietta laughs at something Marcus said, and she tucks a strand of hair behind her ear. Marcus reaches his hand across the table, and when Henrietta takes it, I mumble a curse under my breath.

They look happy.

But where in the world is the reverend?

Once I'm free of the bushes and out of sight of my lying best friend, I whip out my phone and dial Reverend Philip's number.

As it rings into my ear, I hear another phone ringing obnoxiously behind me. When the reverend finally answers, it's as if his voice is…

"Emma Jane, how delightful."

I spin on my heel and come face to face with the handsome man.

Usually handsome.

Right now? Not so much.

His face is flushed, and I can smell the wine wafting off of him in waves.

"Reverend Philip. What are you doing out here instead of in there?" I point to the seafood restaurant.

The tall, muscular man flashes an off-kilter smile and stumbles as he takes a step closer to me. "I don't want to be on a date with that girl. I'd rather take you home for a date."

When he reaches out to touch me, warning bells signal in my head. I swat his hand away, and he has the audacity to laugh. "Oh, don't be like that, Emma Jane. I've seen you looking at me from the pulpit. Don't act like you don't want me the way I desire you."

His slurred speech combined with his audacious words have me taking baby steps backwards. That is, until I'm flat against the brick wall of the restaurant.

"Stop this nonsense, Reverend. You're drunk. We should probably get you home."

"I've loved you for a long time, Emma."

I cringe at his use of just my first name. That's reserved only for Knightley.

"No, you haven't, Reverend. You don't know me at all, and you only think you like me."

He laughs condescendingly then runs his finger down my bare arm.

"I'm very much in love with you. Have been since I first laid eyes on you three years ago. Come home with me." He takes another step forward, so I duck around him and head for my car. Once I'm in with my door shut, I crank it.

Or I try to.

The engine grinds, and then the leering man appears at my window, shouting something about letting him take me home.

My insides have grown ice cold at this point, and I have half the mind to bolt into the restaurant and have Marcus and Henrietta take me home. But they looked so sickeningly happy, and even if I wasn't a fan of Marcus to begin with, I'm definitely his number one advocate after this show the reverend is putting on outside my window.

And I know that the reverend won't actually hurt me. I think.

But regardless, I'll need help stopping him and, well, I'm sort of stranded at the moment.

The elders WILL hear about this.

He knocks on the glass, and I grab my phone, dialing the one person who I know is currently in town and will come to help.

After two rings, he picks up.

"Emma Jane? You know I'm on a—"

"Knightley." His name comes out of my mouth heavy and breathy. "I need help."

"Where are you?"

"Outside of Perry's Seafood. The reverend is here, and he's drunk, and he's trying to touch me and—" He pounds on my window once more, shouting obscenities and looking angrier by the second.

Maybe I am in trouble, but how do I get out of here without him getting me?

"I'm on my way." Knightley's voice is sharp. I keep him on the phone with me, hearing him tell Mallory that he has to go, loud footsteps, and then a muttered curse. "I'm blocked in. Can't get to my truck."

I try to crank mine again, but nothing.

Then I hear nothing but a loud static noise in my ear interrupted by what sounds like heavy breathing.

"Knightley, is everything okay?"

"I'm coming, Emma. Hold on. I'm running as fast as I can."

Two hands splay on my window, and now the reverend has garnered the attention of people exiting the restaurant. With pleading eyes that I pray convey, "someone get this man," I stare at the two men and two women.

One of the women turns around and heads back into the restaurant while the two men approach my car, effectively pulling the reverend's attention away from me. Once the two men coax him away from my car, I get out silently and slip into the restaurant alongside the other older woman. She sits me down in a booth, and that's when Henrietta notices me.

Right as the two women who saw the scene outside ask me if I'm okay and need help, Henrietta and Marcus approach the table. "Emma Jane, are you okay? You look like you've seen a ghost."

I huff. "I wish it were a ghost. The reverend is making a huge scene outside. Did you know he was here?"

Marcus grabs her hand while she looks down at me sheepishly, oblivious to what just occurred outside. "I don't like him, Emma Jane. I like Marcus. I was going to go on this date with him, I swear. But when he showed up, he went off on me saying something about how he wished I was you. Marcus showed up then. He took me inside, ordered us dinner, and I told him that my rejection of his letter was all a big lie."

"I'm so sorry, Henrietta. I should have never put you into this situation. I—" Tears prickle in the corner of my eyes, but I shove them back. I have no right to cry right now. That could have been Henrietta instead of me out there.

Because of me.

"I know, Emma Jane. Thank you for apologizing, and I forgive you. It's okay."

Right as I open my mouth to respond, the door swings open, and the two men who were occupying the reverend stroll inside. "Ma'am, are you okay?"

"Yes, I'm fine," I answer the older gentleman. "Where is the man?"

"The mayor showed up and said he'd take care of it, though he looked all out of sorts."

I shoot to my feet and am out the door in four long strides. I look around, but I don't see the reverend or Knightley. I check over by my car, and there's no one. Then, I hear a yelp, similar to one of a hurt puppy, come from the back of the restaurant. I run around and find Knightley holding the reverend by his black collar, shoving him against the brick building.

"...And if you ever so much as *breathe* in her direction, so help me God, your career as a reverend will not be the only thing you lose."

"Knightley!" He snaps his head to me, and I watch visible relief slink through the reverend's body as he drops his head down to his chest. Marcus and Henrietta appear at my side, and Knightley quickly instructs Marcus to hold the reverend back. Once Marcus has him, Knightley stalks toward me, wrapping me in his arms when he's close enough to touch me. He's sweaty and smelly, but I don't care. He's my safety.

I melt into his arms, and that's when a tear decides to trickle down my cheek.

"You're safe," Knightley whispers against my ear, his large hand holding my head against his racing heart. "I'm going to kill him."

I chuckle then pull back, wiping at the rebellious tear. "No, but we are getting a new leader of our church, right?"

"Absolutely we are," he comments as if he's Dwight from *The Office.* We've watched that entire show together. That little thought of familiarity has me remembering my conversation with Halle from over a week ago. I look into his eyes, and my heart races for a whole new reason. He bailed on his date for me. He ran to me. He showed up for me.

"And I'm calling the police on this sick man," Knightley says, breaking me from the spell I momentarily fell under.

We both look at the reverend, who is slumped down against the wall, barely conscious. Marcus isn't even holding him anymore. Henrietta gives me a questioning look, and I tell her I'll fill her in on everything later. "But for now, can you two get the reverend home? I don't think we need to call the cops. He was drunk and acting stupid."

Part of me wonders if we should tell the police, but the last thing I want to do at this point is give statements. I just want to go home.

As if reading my mind, Knightley nods and repeats my question to Marcus. They agree to drive the now passed out man home.

I pivot toward Knightley, my heart shuddering under his caring gaze.

"You ran to me..."

"You needed me."

KNIGHTLEY

RULE #11: MISTAKES WILL NOT BREAK YOU. IT'S OKAY TO GET A MATCH WRONG. THE IMPORTANT THING IS TO TRY AGAIN.

Emma Jane doesn't know this, but I am going to the police tomorrow. It'll be good that my hot temper has a chance to cool before I storm up into the precinct to demand...

I don't know what I'm demanding, as the reverend never got around to hurting Emma Jane, thank God. Maybe I can convince them he needs a ticket for drunken misconduct? As much as I love the law, it falls short and fails at times because of its reactive nature.

I can see the tiredness and exhaustion from the situation etched across Emma Jane's face, so tonight, I will honor her wishes and take her home.

"There." I close the hood of her car and rub my hands together to get the dust off. "Looks like you have a bad starter switch. I'll get it fixed tomorrow once the parts store opens."

Emma Jane is leaning against her car, chin lifted toward the darkened sky and hands folded across her chest. She lets out a slow breath. "And your truck is still at The Flats, right?"

I nod and reach out my still somewhat dirty hand. "Care for a nighttime walk through town?"

She looks at my hand for a second before sliding her fingers through mine. And at that very moment, I realize I'm holding her hand.

It's what I offered her, but it didn't dawn on me until right now that I've never held her hand.

This isn't friendship. This is intimately *more.* So much more than holding her because she was scared of the movie. Much, much more than her straddling my body when we accidentally fell.

This is intentional comfort stemming from a place of genuine concern to make sure she feels safe, protected, and secure.

I go to release her hand, but she squeezes. I give her a questioning look, but all she does is fix me with a pleading stare. *As if my touch alone is steadying her.*

That's one heck of a dangerous thought to have...

"I'm sorry I ruined your date," she says, though her tone doesn't sound the least bit sorry. She shouldn't be; the reverend was completely out of line.

"You don't have to be sorry. Mallory understood. I'll always be there when you need me." Emma Jane doesn't know that it wasn't a real date. Mallory and I came up with a plan to fake-date each other to see if I could boost my poll numbers. I thought she was crazy to bring up the idea, but I thought, what the heck? If it works, then great. If not, then nothing is truly lost.

Mallory Granger will become my official fake girlfriend in two weeks during the Town Hall address. We have a whole spectacle planned, starting with allowing townsfolk to see us out in public together.

But I haven't told Emma Jane I'm not seeing Mallory in a romantic capacity. She wants things to go well for me, and I don't want to let her down. Nor do I want to be set up on more dates.

We continue in silence for a minute, my heartbeat quickening every time I remember our joined hands. When we pass people on the street, I nod like nothing in the world is going on. They've seen us around town together plenty, but they've never seen me hold her hand.

Because this is a first.

I release her hand, and she doesn't stop me this time. I don't need ridiculous rumors floating around when I'm about to announce my "secret girlfriend" to the town.

"Knightley," she begins as we take to the sidewalk, the sticky air clinging to every ounce of my skin. "Can I..."

I glance over at her. She's chewing on her lip, her gaze cast down. "Go on."

"Can I tell you something that probably sounds extremely conceited and selfish, but I promise it's not?"

"You can always talk to me, Janie."

Her lips twitch upward as I turn my attention back to the route in front of us. We walk alongside Main Street, passing rows of closed stores, nearing her place of work.

"Are you sure you want to listen to me fall to pieces?"

Squeezing her hand, I reply, "I'll put you back together the way you put together your favorite puzzles."

She lets it all out.

"I'm tired of having to be perfect all the time. I think I've been tired of it for a while. I don't want to fake smiles for the town anymore. I don't want to don a dress to church only to have three other women and girls go out and buy it simply because I wore it. There's no room for mistakes. I can't make mistakes, Knightley." Her voice cracks over my name, and I have the urge to wrap my arm around her and tug her close.

I refrain. With great restraint.

She continues before I can respond. "I made a mistake with Henrietta. Two in a row, actually. Frank Weston and Philip Elton are not good men, and I tried to set my pure-of-heart best friend up with them. How did I miss their character flaws when I'm usually spot-on at reading other people?"

"Because you're fracturing, Emma." My voice is a whisper as I speak my thoughts. I meant to keep that one in my head, but when it comes to the woman beside me, I have a bad habit of blurting. Everyone else in town treats her like a sensitive flower, while I know she can handle the truth. "Perfection is not an achievable standard. No one can keep a mask on for that long and survive."

I think back to Cami and the many times she broke down in my arms over this very thing. Over feeling like she couldn't be authentic because everyone expected too much from her. But where Cami stood her ground and allowed herself room to make mistakes, Emma Jane is too prideful to do that. She can't bear to be seen as a failure.

"What will people say about me when they've learned I've screwed up royally with Henrietta? We easily swept Frank under the rug, but this? This affects all of Hartfield. Our church is the only one in the town."

I cut my eyes to her, pausing in front of a closed boutique. "That's selfish thinking. Who cares what people think? What matters is that the scum of a man is pulled from the position so we can find a real Godly man to lead us as a congregation."

"I know, I know." She starts to walk, but I tug her back, staring into her steel-colored eyes.

"No, Emma. Listen to me. It does not matter what the people of Hartfield, Mississippi, think about you. It doesn't matter if you make a mistake. It doesn't matter if you make a million mistakes. Life is simply not about you. It's not about me. It's about Jesus, plain and simple. All that we do, we do it for Him. Living for yourself only brings heartache and unreachable expectations. Living for Him brings freedom from faultlessness."

She groans and turns away, walking ahead with stiff, raised shoulders. "I know that, Knightley. I do. But I forget it sometimes, you know? When I have every eye on me at church or when I walk through the community or when I'm invited over for dinners or made to host a dinner. Papa needs me all the time, and I can't leave him to be on my own like my sister did. I'm twenty-three, but I feel like I've lived ten lifetimes."

"You've put the pressure on yourself, Emma Jane." I'm at my normal walking speed, so she must be speed walking for my stride to match hers right now. "No one asked you to say yes to every dinner or to wear the prettiest outfits to church so that you can distract every unattached man in the building."

She stops in her tracks. I grab her arm firmly and spin her around, catching her other arm. I lean down so that we are eye to eye. "No one asked you to be perfect."

"They didn't have to. I have to make it up. All of it."

"Make up for what, Emma?"

"Killing my mom!"

Her words steal my breath as she breaks into sobs. No longer caring who sees, I pull her into my arms, holding her tight and silently praying God will remove this burden from her life. I should have known she was suffering inside, but I always chalked her attitude up to her desire to be loved by being perfect. That's a whole other issue; the roots apparently run deep into guilt.

We stand there for a few minutes before she steps away, puffy-eyed with a red, drippy nose. She fishes for tissues somewhere deep in her white crossbody bag. After taking care of her business, we begin to walk again. We're close to where I left my truck, which is hopefully unblocked now. Running that half-mile from The Flats to Perry's Seafood felt like nothing. I had a one-track mind: save Emma Jane. But now, my legs are stiff and my chest aches since the adrenaline has worn off.

"I know your logic is broken right now, but you did not kill your mother, Emma Jane. You know that deep down. Please work on releasing the guilt you harbor."

"I can try. I think that's all I have to offer at the moment."

"Trying is enough." We round a street corner, and I catch sight of my truck, gloriously free with no other vehicles around it. Beside me, Emma Jane snickers. "Do you think people got a video of you running through town?"

"I'll find a way to work it for the campaign. 'Knightley's running to continue making Juniper Grove a better place to live' or something like that."

"Lame. You could headline it: 'When the city needs a hero, Knightley's on the run!'"

"That's so much worse." We laugh—a sound I'm grateful to hear out of her—as we approach my truck. I open the door for Emma Jane, and she plants one sneaker on the lift, hoisting herself up. Just as she twists to sit down, she slips. As I catch her in my arms, she wraps her legs around my waist and her arms around my neck as if she's a koala and I'm her tree. But the momentum from the fall is strong gravity, so as she clings to me, I dip down to absorb the impact, which causes those pretty pink lips that confessed a load tonight to hurtle toward me...

Landing right onto my shocked, open mouth.

My first thought is an explicit curse of pain as our teeth clank together.

My second thought knocks the breath from my lungs as if Emma Jane's fall didn't already accomplish that.

I'm kissing her. Emma Jane.

Right on the mouth.

And outside of the salty blood on my tongue, I like it.

Henry is going to kill me...

Emma Jane

RULE #12: "THERE ARE NO MISTAKES, ONLY HAPPY ACCIDENTS." - BOB ROSS

Two weeks ago, I kissed Knightley Austen for the first time.

Though kiss isn't the right word I should use to describe the encounter. I accidentally attacked him with my mouth after his truck rejected me from entering. Our teeth clinked together, his nose went into my eye, and our foreheads bounced off of one another.

It's what happened AFTER that chaotic episode that still has me reeling.

He didn't push me off.

In fact, his hands slid from my back to hold me up from underneath, and he closed his eyes and sighed.

Sighed!

Right into my open mouth.

And it wasn't a groan of pain. It sounded like pleasure...

It was in that exact moment I learned something new about myself. You see, I never understood the appeal of kissing, much less anything more. I had kissed a total of two guys, and they were good kisses according to Lucy, my romance-loving friend. This kiss was anything but a normal definition of good, but my body reacted as if it was.

Tingled. Wanted *more.*

I was teetering on the edge of letting that feeling take over, but thankfully, the salty, metallic taste of blood erased the desire.

The ride back to my house was roaring with awkward silence. Mostly because both of our lips were bleeding, so we had old napkins from a restaurant I had shoved away in my purse pressed to our faces. He dropped me off at the house and then left without saying another word.

And for the past two weeks, anytime we unintentionally bump into each other (not physically—we haven't gotten remotely close enough to one another for that to happen), our topics of conversation revolve around three things:

One, the weather. (It's like taking a shower from hell outside.)

Two, the election. (He's still performing with lower poll numbers than Jay regardless of becoming *extra* small-town famous for running down Main Street to stop the bad man from hurting the damsel in distress, i.e., me.)

Three, his dates with Mallory. (He seems to enjoy being with her, so I've kept my feelings locked down tightly.)

The bell above the door sounds, so I rise from my elbow-propped position on the barista counter. Knightley strolls in, waving to customers and showing off his suave smile as usual. When he's at the counter and turns his full attention on me, the smile dissipates as if it was only a figment of imagination.

"Americano?" I ask, already reaching for the twenty-four-ounce to-go cup. He nods, then places both hands on the counter.

"Janie?"

His low-toned use of the nickname only he calls me startles me, and I end up spilling espresso beans all over the floor.

That's a future Janie problem, however.

"Hm?" I go about my business, collecting more beans. Why is he affecting me like this all of a sudden? Sure, I made him pretend to marry me when I was five and he was eighteen, but what little girl doesn't do that with the trusted older men in her life? Heck, before it was him, I said I was going to marry my dad.

See?

Little Janie can't be trusted.

Gah, quit calling yourself that! Say it with me: Emma. Jane.

The point is that Knightley has never had this hold on me. He's never made me lose my balance or drop things. That's for the clumsy romance heroines Lucy writes. Not me.

"I'm going to ask Mallory to officially become my girlfriend."

The monster that arose from my soul when I saw her get out of his truck that night makes the briefest of reappearances before I force her down.

Yes, she's a her.

And I think I'll call her Mother Gothel. It's fitting. Selfish, conniving Mother Gothel.

"Congratulations." I'm speaking, but the voice belongs to someone else entirely.

Mother Gothel, probably.

I'm not doing a great job of keeping her at bay.

I focus on making his drink while he talks.

"Thank you. Why don't you go ahead and use our story for your website?"

After taking a steadying breath—okay, more like five—I turn to him with his Americano in hand. When he takes it from me, our fingers brush, as they have a gazillion times in the past.

But this time, the heat from the coffee cup somehow spreads into my chest.

"That's a great idea." I paste a smile on my face as I stare at the man who admittedly becomes more handsome each time I see him. His beard is full and trimmed. Hair styled back effortlessly. Don't get me started on the way he fills out that cream, collared shirt. And there's a faint mark remaining on his bottom lip where my tooth stuck him two weeks ago.

Does he look at it and think of me?

Oh, dear good and glorious things above, Emma Jane. Why are you thinking that? He probably sees it and hopes I never get that close to him again.

Age gap. He's the mayor of a whole town. He's practically family. He likes Mallory. Thinks she's pretty. Wants to make things official with her.

Brunette and brown-eyed. Tall. Slim.

Whereas I'm short. Platinum blonde and gray-eyed. Have man-shoulders and thick thighs. I can even grow a mustache! Thanks again, PCOS.

"I'll ask her to email you her statement tonight after our date." And with that, he takes his coffee, and I watch his fine butt—it's those navy dress pants, friend—walk out of the building as if he didn't just pull the pin from a grenade and set it on the counter to detonate.

The urge to go to battle consumes me, and I stop myself from marching out that door with trumpets blaring and drums beating to get him to turn around and see me.

See me as more than what I am.

More than I believe myself to be.

I like him. It's worse now that I realize I like him.

But he's unattainable.

And now he's unavailable.

Did I lose my chance by not laying all my cards on the table?

"Emma Jane, dear. Is everything okay?" Mr. Sam, the elderly owner of Books and Beans, hobbles to the counter. I zoned so far out I didn't hear him come in. He looks at me with concern in his light brown eyes, his bushy gray eyebrows raised.

"Of course, Mr. Sam. What brings you in today? Can I make you some tea?"

"Yes, dear." He slowly makes his way over to sit down in one of the comfy chairs by the bookstacks. I make his typical herbal green tea then walk it over to him, sitting down in the chair beside him since no one is in the cafe at the moment.

"How have you been? It's been a couple of weeks since I've seen you."

He blows softly on his tea. "My daughter came down for a visit and is insisting I move down south with her. Says I can't get along by myself." He harrumphs. "Told her I can't up and leave this place."

I nod along as he talks, trying not to let my brain entertain the idea of owning this place. I have countless ideas on how to make this place even better than it is, and Mr. Sam has allowed me to implement some of them, like the incandescent lights and replacing the walls with floor-to-ceiling windows. But I don't ever want to overstep my position as manager. His soul is connected to this place through his deceased wife.

"Have you thought about selling, Mr. Sam?"

He grunts, but it's not an angry grunt. More of an "I don't want to face that thought" grunt. He finally says, "I want to make sure I have the right person to sell to."

A spark of excitement forms within me. "What if you sold it to me?"

He eyes me warily. "You can afford to buy it?"

"Yes," I say confidently. I know Papa would think this is a good investment and would help me out. "And I would continue the great work you've accomplished here."

"Eh, I don't know, Emma Jane. I don't know if my heart is ready to let it go."

"I understand, Mr. Sam. Until you are ready, just know I'll continue taking care of Books and Beans with my whole heart, okay? I love this place. Friends, families, strangers, and lovers connect here. It's a beautiful and magical place in our town."

In a rare show of affection, Mr. Sam smiles and places his hand on my shoulder. "That it is, Emma Jane. That it is."

"Well done, Emma Jane. Your app is simple enough that even an old lady like me could join if I chose to."

I clasp my hands together, eyes growing wide as I stare up at Jane Austen.

"You could be my next beta member! Since it's worked so well for your son and all." The twinge of bitterness in my voice is drowned out by my excitement over the idea of matching Jane with an eligible man.

"If I chose to," she reiterates, giving me a pointed glare. Her white hair is styled into a neat bun on top of her head, and her clothing is shades of brown and black. She resembles Professor McGonagall from *Harry Potter,* and the thought crosses my mind that I could run theme dates through the app for people who enjoy the same fandoms.

"So choose to."

Jane laughs and then begins to massage my shoulders. I groan as I feel the tension I've carried since "that night" release, loving that she's the kind of woman who will tend to your needs without having to ask. Jane is like a mother to me. Between her and Halle, I have been well taken care of, and the thought puts me at ease. When I miss my biological mom, though I never knew her, remembering I have these two ladies in my life comforts me.

"I'll put 'gives an outstanding massage' on your profile." I moan as her thumb digs into my shoulder. "You'll have a match in no time."

Jane chuckles and spends a few more minutes working my neck and shoulders before she moves to sit across from me in the sitting room. "You found my son a match, did you? He hasn't mentioned it to me."

"Her name is Mallory Granger, and she's a wonderful woman..." Gosh, I hate myself right now. Jealousy saturates my system like deadly snake venom.

Jane is silent, her brows pinched in contemplation. "Are you sure they are an item? Knightley's not one to keep secrets from me, but I do think he'd wait until he knew for sure to tell me."

"He's going to ask her to make things official tonight."

"Emma Jane, I have a serious question for you, and I want you to be honest with me, okay? Don't let the fact that I'm his mother determine your answer." Jane fixes me with a hard stare—an expression her son wears when he's about to chastise me—her hands splaying on my desk.

I swallow a building lump in my throat and nod.

"Do you like Knightley?"

Choking on a laugh, I cough a few times before answering. "Of course I like him. He's my biggest nuisance at times, but he's also my very best guy friend. I look up to him and respect him and—"

"That's not what I mean, E. J. You know that."

I only admitted it to myself a few weeks ago. Trust me, I've tried to get rid of the feelings. They hang around like a disastrous stain on my favorite shirt. Now God wants me to speak these ridiculous feelings aloud to his mother?

Nope.

"If you are asking if I like Knightley romantically, then I can truly say..." Gah. I can't blatantly lie to this woman. She knows me too well, and I respect her too greatly. "Yes. Unfortunately, I do. But I'll get over it, don't worry. I'm not even sure how it happened." I take a sip of water to cool my burning face.

"You straddled him on the kitchen floor is what happened."

Water dribbles down my chin as I choke on the liquid. After wiping my mouth, I meet her amused expression. "That was an accident!"

She shrugs her delicate shoulders. "Accident or not, it still happened. And I was certain I'd have to drag your father out of the room so you two could kiss."

"The thought never crossed my mind!" Which is true. I felt... something. But it wasn't a desire to kiss him. It was more like a warm, fuzzy feeling enveloping me. I wanted to lay on top of him and hug him. I wanted to be ensnared in his arms. I wanted to never detach myself from him.

But kiss?

No way.

Not until that accidental one... "What's with me and accidents?"

"Hm?" Jane asks as I mumble.

Might as well come clean to her. About *everything*.

"We accidentally kissed two weeks ago." I wring my hands in my lap, wondering if she's pushing *for* us or *against* us.

There's no us, I remind myself.

"Interesting. And how did you manage to *accidentally* liplock with my son?" Her tone isn't upset, angry, or disappointed. She's... curious. Her blue eyes sparkle with eager excitement.

"I slipped getting into his truck—you know how lifted that monstrosity is—and when he caught me, my lips smashed into his. It wasn't pretty. There was blood." I chuckle, hoping she doesn't ask how—

"How did you feel about it?"

Gosh darn it. "I wanted more. More lips. Less teeth. Definitely less blood."

"I see." Jane hums, then she fixes me with a serious stare. "Pray tell, Emma Jane—" My insides flip at the phrase Knightley uses. Guess I know where he got it from now. "—my sweet girl who carries my name, why did you set him up with another woman?"

Time to take her through my internal laundry list. "He's thirteen years older than me. We grew up together. He was married to Cami, who was like an older sister to me. I'm never getting married because I—" I stop myself just short of telling her that my chances of having kids are slim to none because of my disease.

"Finish the sentence, dear. Tell me everything. Because the reasons you've listed prior are not valid excuses in my book."

Tears well in my eyes, but I shove them down as I gather the courage to tell her my deepest secret. Will she think less of me? Think of me as less of a woman? Halle and Henrietta didn't think that of me when I told them, but the only reason they know is because Halle was the one to take me to the appointments, and Henrietta was spending the week at a summer camp with me a few years ago when I had a flare. I've never outright told somebody because, well, it makes me imperfect, and that's not what's expected of me.

No one asked you to be perfect. Knightley's words come back to me full force. He asked me to try and resolve the ridiculous guilt I carry over my mother's death. And I have been trying over the past two weeks. When I feel the need to be perfect, I remind myself that no one asked me to be, and I'm not at fault for my mother's passing.

Taking a steadying breath and wiping a stray tear, I decide to be brave. I can trust Jane, and she's the perfect person to practice vulnerability with. "I was diagnosed with polycystic ovary syndrome, or PCOS, when I was fifteen." There. It's out.

"Oh, honey." Jane stands, and I meet her in the middle of the room, welcoming her warm, tight embrace. "Why didn't you tell me?"

Through small, muffled cries—my face is planted in her cotton t-shirt—I reply, "I was scared. I may never be able to have kids, Jane. I can't continue to harbor feelings for your son because I can't give him the future he desires."

"Sweet girl," she says as she pulls back. Her hands never leave my arms. "I can't speak for him, but I can say without hesitation that you'll never know unless you open your mouth and ask."

"Easier said than done." I laugh without mirth. "Besides, the other reasons are valid to me. I can't make a move on Knightley. What if he laughs at me? Or pats my head like I'm a child and tells me it's just a phase? I can't risk that kind of humiliation."

After a pause, I add, "He's making things official with Mallory tonight. I cannot and will not get in the way of a relationship regardless of how I feel."

Finally, Jane nods as if she understands. "Did you know your mother had PCOS?"

A dammed wall inside me breaks, and the tears I was working so hard to push back come flooding out. My mom had this same disease? Yet she bore me and my sister. Though I killed her.

No, Emma Jane. You didn't kill her. "Did she die giving birth to me because of a complication from PCOS?"

Jane nods solemnly. "Preeclampsia. Your father never told you?"

I shake my head. "He doesn't like talking about it."

"Stubborn man," Jane mumbles under her breath as she pulls me into another hug.

PCOS killed her.

And it could kill me, too, if I was blessed to become pregnant.

All the more reason to never get married.

All the more reason to let Knightley go.

KNIGHTLEY

RULE #13: MATCHES OF THE HEART AND MIND ARE JUST AS IMPORTANT AS A MATCH ON PAPER.

"Our next question comes from Hadley Rawls, the local owner of Southern Grace Boutique and Gift Market, whose boutique and jewelry brand has spread regionally from right here in Juniper Grove. Mrs. Rawls would like to know each of your plans to not only support and promote small businesses, but also how each of you will help new business startups in the area. She'd like to know your plans on local taxing, bringing down building rent prices, and drawing more consumers into brick-and-mortar stores through town beautification."

City councilman, Harry Ladner, sets the microphone down as he motions for democratic candidate, John Lowe, to speak first. This is our final Town Hall Address of the election cycle, and frankly, I'm glad it's almost over.

Even if my polls are still down by two percent in favor of the man standing to my left, Jansen Johnson. Honestly, at this point, I'd be okay if he wins. Throughout these Q&A sessions, he's impressed me.

But I'm also not a man who will lie down and roll over. I'll fight for this position until the end. Just to see my commitment through.

As Jay takes his time answering, I look out over the small audience gathered. Many more town members are watching and commenting online, but the meeting room is full of business owners, school representatives, bigwigs of the catfishing industry, and then there are the average men and women who are concerned and involved citizens of the city.

When my turn to answer approaches, I note how I've spent the past four years as mayor of Juniper Grove working to make our city a beautiful college town, which in turn has attracted more entrepreneurs. I speak to my history of fighting to lower rent prices and of lowering local taxes so that we could continue to grow as a town. I make a vow to continue my work if reelected.

Questions continue to pour in, and for the next half hour, we take turns answering with various levels of applause as a response. The poor democratic candidate gets minimal applause, and I kind of feel bad for the guy. It's hard to run on that ticket in Mississippi, regardless if you're a neutral-leaning Democrat or not. Eventually, Councilman Ladner hands the mic off to the president of the local Baptist association, Pastor Vance Green. The slightly overweight man who is around my age moves to stand in front of the black podium.

"As the president of the Baptist association of this county, I feel the need to call into question some religious aspects of the candidates." He gives me a pointed stare, and I inwardly sigh. *Here we go.* I figured he'd put forth this line of questioning tonight, which is why it's the perfect time for me and Mallory to become official to the town. It's all a ruse, of course, but I'm committed to the plan now. I couldn't tell Emma Jane the truth; she wanted to use us and our "success" for her website. But I also couldn't surprise her with the rest of the town, so I told Emma Jane on Friday I was asking Mallory because she needed to know beforehand.

Why did I feel like she needed to know beforehand?

No clue.

"I wasn't the president four years ago when our current mayor was elected to office, but I was vocal about my doubts. You see, the Bible says…"

Vance Greene rambles on about a particular verse in the Book of First Timothy that speaks specifically to being a deacon. However, he attempts to twist the language to insist it also refers to politicians. Last election cycle he was simply an annoyance, but this year, he has a bigger platform. He was appointed to the position for a reason, though it escapes me.

"Mayor Austen, do you care to answer to the community regarding your theological views or stance on leadership as a grown, *single* man?"

The door opens, and Emma Jane walks through. My stomach drops. *Where is—*

Mallory walks in behind Emma Jane, and a smile lights my face at the sight of her. *Thank heavens!* I thought she'd bailed on me for a minute there. She was supposed to enter before Vance Green got started.

"I completely disagree with your reading of First Timothy. It does not apply to leadership spheres outside of the church. There is no scriptural evidence for such things. In fact, Paul recommends singleness if one can attain it. Have you read that, Pastor?" I pause for effect, but he only huffs. I continue, "And I'd like to take this time to remind everyone of all the good I've done as a single man governing this town. Regardless of my theological opinions, you're deafeningly wrong in one respect, Pastor Green. I do have a girlfriend. We've been dating quietly, and we are now ready to become public." I gesture to the back of the room. "Everyone, I'd like for you to meet Mallory Granger."

Heads turn and follow the pretty, confident brunette as she strides to my side, slipping one arm around my waist and planting a light kiss on my cheek. I offer a thankful smile.

I wish I felt something by this intimate contact, but there's nothing.

When I catch sight of Emma Jane's back walking out of the door, however, I'm flooded with guilt and a pressing desire to chase her down and tell her it's all fake.

Would she be upset? *Would she be happy?*

Why would she be relieved and happy that it's fake? It's not like she wants me as anything more than her older friend. She'd probably think me gross if she knew some of the thoughts I've had about her recently. Especially after we had that atrocious kiss.

It was bad, by all accounts.

But I wanted to try again. This time, not accidentally. I almost made it real in the moment. I was drawn to her like a moth to a flame. Closed my eyes and let out a whimpered sigh and everything. It was out of my control.

The blood and her groaning pain stopped me and brought me back to my senses.

I shove the thoughts from my mind and focus on the rest of the Town Hall address, answering questions (which now heavily focus on my new "relationship"), noting the progress I've made in the city over the past four years, and hitting my talking points for what I will continue to do moving forward.

EMMA JANE

RULE #14: WAITING FOR THE RIGHT "PERFECT MOMENT" CAN BITE YOU IN THE BUTT. ALLOW YOUR CLIENTS TO GO ROGUE SOMETIMES.

I once thought Jane Austen was on my side but that notion is shattered glass on the ground, much like the plate I dropped onto the hardwood floor ten minutes ago.

"Why must I be here tonight?" I ask, setting the long, red oak table with her finest, floral-patterned china. I matched Knightley and Mallory, so I don't necessarily need to 'get to know them' more.

"To show your support," Jane reiterates for the thousandth time. "You sat on your chance to tell him how you feel."

"I never had the chance! We had our conversation after he informed me he was asking her to be his girlfriend, if you recall."

Jane pegs me with a look and swishes her hand in front of her face. "No, ma'am. This is on you, sweet child. You could have told him before our conversation."

I have no comeback because she is justified as always.

The front door to Killington Mansion, Knightley's childhood home, opens, but the kitchen is not in sight of the foyer. Creaks in the floorboard echo through the house as the guest approaches the kitchen. Before long, a voice I know—rich and deep—says, "You've outdone yourself, Mom. The food smells amazing." He rounds the corner, and I whirl away from him and busy myself straightening the edge of the white lace table runner since my emotions won't dissipate from my face. I feel the frown, the heaviness in my chest, and the pinch of my brows. But no matter how hard I try, I can't fix my face into a welcoming expression, much less a blank one.

What's happening to my control?

He approaches me from behind, and my back warms from the late-September Mississippi heat radiating in waves off of him, much stronger than the normal heat he puts off when he's near me. He must have been at my father's place and walked over here. "Thank you for helping my mom out."

I inhale deeply before turning to meet him; he steps back as I move. "Of course. I'll always be around to help Jane with insignificant dinners such as this one."

His blue eyes bore into me, a flash of indignation crossing them. "Insignificant?" He sputters a laugh before grabbing my forearm and dragging me out of the dining area, through the kitchen, where Jane watches with a smirk on her face, and then into the hallway before going through a swinging door and landing in his father's old office. "Let me remind you, lest you forget, you wanted this. You matched me and Mallory together. You set up the date. You said I needed to do this. You said it would help your business."

I cross my arms, refusing to meet his eyes. I can't control the pout in my voice when I speak. "Yes, and?"

Knightley lets out another laugh of disbelief as he runs his hand down his face. "Now you're upset and angry at me for following your wishes? I don't understand you, Emma Jane."

He waits for me to respond, but when I remain silent, staring out of the old dusty window toward the backyard garden, he stalks out of the room, the door swinging closed behind him. The sound ricochets around my head.

I collapse onto the mustard brown settee, a cloud of dust billowing around me as I inwardly scream. What's wrong with me? What happened to my control? Why can't I bring myself to fake a smile or even tap into my snarky charm?

Jealousy swims in my veins. It's like a flesh-eating bacteria, eroding me from the inside out. "God, please help me," I cry out through falling tears. I don't want to feel this way. I want to be happy for my friend. "Take these feelings from me." I want him to be happy. I don't want to lose him. The only way to never lose him is to make him mine forever. But that opportunity has sailed on the *S. S. Mallory.*

Knightley is right. I caused this. I set him up on the ridiculous premise I could use him for my endeavors. I tried to force Henrietta into the arms of not one but two awful, no-good men. All because I matched one couple who already liked each other, as Knightley once pointed out. Why am I like this? Calculating and... and...

Manipulative.

The word bites my skin, and I cringe.

I don't mean to be, but I—

I just want people to like me.

Shaking the thought away because it feels like a thousand pounds crushing down on my chest, I turn my attention back to matchmaking.

Why did I want to start this business anyway?

The ugly truth rings out clearly as I search my heart for the answer: I want something more than living off of Papa's money, working at Books and Beans, and pleasing the entire town of Hartfield.

I love my job at Books and Beans, but I can't stay there, never moving up and challenging myself. I need a challenge. There are only so many coffee combinations I can create. I want a challenge in business practices. I want to take the coffee shop and bookstore to a new level. But I can't because it's not mine to change.

Papa is a whole other situation. I have to be there for him, and I will not bail on taking care of him. I will not place him in a nursing home. I want to stay with him until he's no longer with me. I love him. He sacrificed so much to raise me and Bella, and this is the least I can do for him. I cannot and will not leave him.

And Hartfield.

I love this small town. I love the antebellum homes that spaciously line this road. I love our church. I love the people. I love them so much I've strived to be their town gem, their southern belle, their debutante princess as they've wanted me to be.

Did they want it?

Or did I do it for myself? Out of my insecurities that I'm not enough for the people around me? That I have to make up for the death of my mother?

It's as if my entire paradigm is shifting, and the perfect control I once held is slipping through my fingertips, preparing to shatter on the floor at the right moment.

"**M**allory, you are a precious soul. How did Knightley get so lucky to snag you up?" Mary Bates's voice is like nails on a chalkboard. Not to mention the current content of her speech.

Mallory laughs, tucking a strand of brown hair behind her ear. Her silver earrings are bows, and I don't know if I'm more jealous over her fashion sense or her relationship with Knightley.

"Well, we have Emma Jane to thank, of course."

The table applauds, and I want to crawl under the long, wooden rectangle and hide like a child trying to sneak dessert before the main course.

But instead, I paste on a smile and nod my head as if I'm winning an award. When I catch Henrietta's eyes, she flashes me a weird look. Like she's uncomfortable. She glances away and whispers something in Marcus's ear.

"I'm glad she got this match right. Our poor Henrietta went through not one but two failed matches because of Emma Jane. Not to mention both men were sleazes. Can you believe that so-called *reverend* said those nasty things to my Henrietta when he decided not to date her because she wasn't Emma Jane?" With every word that Henrietta's aunt continues to speak, recounting the awful behavior of our former reverend, my stomach sinks into a pit of despair. All eyes at the table flick to me, and as Mrs. Bates continues to spew from the mouth, their expressions go from curious to disbelief and settle on shame.

Or is it because I feel shame in my gut that I believe everyone is looking at me in that capacity? It's too much to bear. Their stares, Mrs. Bates's high-pitched shrill, the disappointed look from the red-headed man sitting across from me. Henrietta's sympathetic expression.

How does she carry sympathy for me? Mrs. Bates is right. I did this, I—

I can't breathe.

All of the thoughts from before dinner come barreling back to me.

As I stand, my chair falls. The noise of it crashing to the ground reminds me of the sound I'm making as I fall from the pedestal I've stood upon for years. This is it. This is the moment where everyone discovers I am not perfect. Where everyone disowns me and shuns me. Where I lose everything I've tried to maintain. Where I become unloved. Where my castle crumbles and my reign comes to an end.

I've let everyone down. Put my best friend into awful situations with awful men.

All because I needed to be perfect. Needed to make people like me and see my worth.

"Enough!" Henrietta's voice booms from the opposite end of the table. She stands, slamming her hands on the table. The table quiets, but I don't have the strength to rip my gaze from my black, sparkly shoes. She clears her throat. "Emma Jane has apologized to me, and I have forgiven her. Aunt Mary, you have no right to give a tongue lashing to my friend like this. I told you before we left the house for this dinner to not peep a word. We will talk about this further at home."

"Child, how dare you—"

"No." Henrietta's voice is firm. "At home."

I hear chairs scratching against the floor, and then Henrietta is at my side. I gather enough courage to meet her eyes. She smiles and pulls me into a hug. "I love you, E. J. Please don't take what she said to heart."

As she walks away, tears stream down my face. What did I do to deserve a friend like her? I don't deserve her, and that is the truth of the matter.

Henrietta leaves, dragging Mrs. Bates with her. Marcus waves goodbye before following them out. Halle and Grant say their goodbyes. Mallory pulls Knightley to the side while Jane comes around to embrace me. I crumble in her arms, sobbing uncontrollably. "She's right, Jane. I don't deserve the love of this town. She's right to call me out. I didn't know Frank and Elton were the way that they are. I swear it. I never would do something to intentionally hurt Henrietta. She knows that, right? She says she does, but does she really?" I can't bring myself to voice my thoughts from earlier. Not to Jane. I have to work through these character flaws on my own. With God. And pray I'm forgiven for my mindless mistakes in desperate attempts to be enough.

My words are jumbled and broken between trying to catch my breath and speak my heart. Jane pats my back, whispering in my ear, "You're okay, Emma Jane. You're okay. She knows."

I stop trying to talk and cry in her arms until the tears start to run dry. Knightley brings a box of tissues over, telling his mom that Mallory left, and we all three sit down at the table as I blow my nose and dry my face. Moments pass as I shut my thoughts down, trying to collect myself.

The front door opens, and someone walks in, but I can't bring myself to look up.

"Can you give us a moment?" It's Henrietta's voice. Jane and Knightley must agree because they get up and leave the room. When she places her hand on my thigh, the deluge resumes.

"Henrietta, I am so sorry. I never meant to try and set you up with pitiful men. Had I known their colors, I never would have—"

"Shh." She continues making a gentle shushing sound even as I cry. "I know you didn't. I didn't know either."

"But you did," I continue sobbing, trying to get my words out. "I should have listened to you about Elton Philip after the first date went disastrously. I'm so sorry, Henrietta. You are my best friend, and I was being completely selfish."

"I forgive you, E. J. I forgave you when you apologized after the incident with *him*."

I hug my best friend, and she begins to cry. We both hold each other, crying, until we can't anymore.

"Why are you crying?" I ask, trying to laugh to lighten the mood.

"Because my best friend is," she exclaims, grabbing a tissue and blotting her eyes. "What's going on, E. J.? This," she sweeps her hand up and down my frame, "surely isn't all about me."

"I don't know, Hen. I'm just..." I pause, taking a deep breath. "I'm a mess. I need to tell you something, but I can't say it here. Not right now. Do you want to go for a drive or something?"

"I'd love to. I'll drive and drop you off when we get back from wherever we end up. Then I'll go deal with my aunt. I'm so sorry she said those things about you."

I sigh. "She wasn't all wrong, you know."

"Regardless. It wasn't her place. Not at a happy little gathering like tonight was supposed to be."

Henrietta stands, tugging me to my feet. I follow her out of the house before remembering I left my purse in the sitting room.

When I open the door, Knightley is standing there as if he was going to walk outside. "Um, excuse me. I'll just—" I try to scoot around him, but he steps in front of me.

"Are you okay, Emma Jane?"

"I will be okay," I say, not meeting his eyes.

"I'm here for you." His voice is a pained whisper, and after a beat, I gather the courage to look at him. His blue eyes are dark, his jaw set.

I manage a soft smile, my heart breaking as I say, "You can't be. Not anymore."

KNIGHTLEY

"Where's your better half?" Stone Harper, the director and founder of the Juniper Grove Community Center, asks. He approached my campaign booth at the Juniper Grove Sweet Tea Festival minutes ago to make sure I received his invite to the Halloween Bash the center is putting on for Halloween in a little over a week.

I scratch the back of my neck. "She's working, but she'll drop by here after."

Stone nods, his blond hair catching in the slight wind, then glances back at his girlfriend, who is chatting with Emma Jane by some booth set up for a friendship bracelet exchange.

Why is that a trend?

Should I have "Knightley for Mayor" friendship bracelets made to appeal to younger voters?

I cringe. Nope. Not happening.

"Hey, have you thought of how we could go about a community-wide Fourth of July fireworks display?" Stone asks, his blue eyes widening with excitement. "We have this event back in Dasher Valley, and it'd be cool to have one here, too." He continues to tell me all about the logistics of the event and how he thinks we could transfer something similar to Juniper Grove. We continue to chat for a few minutes before his girlfriend and Emma Jane approaches.

"Mayor, have you met my girlfriend, Lucy Spence?" Stone asks, slipping his arm around her, though his smile as he looks down at her doesn't quite meet his eyes. When she gazes up at him, there is... fear? Concern? Sadness?

Should I look deeper into this? Surely Stone wouldn't be hurting a girl, right?

I exchange a quick look with Emma Jane, trying to have a silent conversation with her, but she turns her head and looks everywhere else. I reach out my hand to shake Lucy's. "Nice to meet you, Miss Spence. Emma Jane has told me a lot about you, and of course, I'd recognize a lady that looks like my former employee, Lorelei, anywhere. I hear you're our local romance author?"

She chuckles, but the sound is weak. She's ghostly pale beneath her freckles. I cut my eyes toward Stone, who wears a worried expression. Maybe she's just sick today or something. I need to stop reading political thrillers.

"That's me." She smiles once more, but it's... haunted. She rises onto her toes and whispers in Stone's ear, and then the two of them say their goodbyes, leaving me and Emma Jane alone at the tent.

"Emma Jane." Once she looks at me instead of organizing the pamphlets on the fold-out table, I ask, "Is everything okay with Lucy? Is Stone... hurting her somehow?"

"What?" She throws her hands onto her hips. "Not a chance. Though I have noticed Lucy hasn't been quite the same lately. She says it's because of a book deadline or something."

"All right, well. I trust you."

"We need more water." Gerald and Fred, the two guys helping with today's campaign stuff, approach.

"I'll go purchase some," Emma Jane offers, and the guys take a seat in the shade.

I watch as Emma Jane leaves, wondering if she's having a better day. The past month since everything went down at Mom's house, she's been different. More standoffish, but not mean or rude. Just reclusive, I guess. Some days her smile is genuine while other days it's forced.

But no matter how much I press, she won't tell me what's wrong. And when I ask Marcus if he has heard anything from Henrietta, he tells me that Emma Jane is working through stuff but she's okay.

I wish she would let me be there for her. Like she has in the past. Except...

I've never cared this much. Have never had her on my mind as I fall asleep. Or typed and deleted text messages over and over. Or prayed to God that He would destroy whatever mental monsters she's facing that she won't share with me.

"People sound like they're voting for you, you know? I know the poll numbers haven't been great, but word of mouth says otherwise." Gerald claps me on the back, pulling me out of my thoughts.

We get back to work, handing out informational pamphlets; talking to friends, strangers, and people visiting for the festival; and giving cotton candy and stickers to kids who come up to my booth. When Emma Jane returns with the waters, the men set off, and she decides to tag along with them to, quote, "try to reach younger voters for me."

As the festival comes to an end, Emma Jane sticks around to help me pack up. Mallory was supposed to be here by now, but she hasn't shown up. We have a reservation for dinner at The Flats tonight, and we were supposed to leave from here together.

"Looking for your girlfriend?" Emma Jane questions, following my gaze to the parking lot. Her tone is more gentle than in the past, and it eats me alive. I want to tell her it's all a farce. I'm not in love with Mallory, and she's not in love with me. I don't know why I even went along with this, and now I feel stuck.

It's not like I have anyone else available to me, though.

The election is a little under three weeks away, and then we can naturally come to an end. No one needs to know this arrangement was for anything short of us liking each other.

"We have a date tonight," I say. Emma Jane nods her head, but I don't miss the frown on her face. In an instant, she shifts it to a smile, however, and begins to collect pamphlets that had fallen onto the ground. I set down the *Knightley for Mayor* stickers I'm holding and grab her shoulders, spinning her around to face me. "Emma Jane, what are you hiding from me? Ever since Mom hosted the dinner party for me and Mallory last month, you've been off."

She averts her gray eyes, her fingers tugging at the hem of her sparkly black shirt. A sure sign of nervousness for her. *Why is she nervous?*

"I'm fine."

"That's the biggest lie you've ever told," I scoff but grow serious. "Tell me. What's bothering you? Why have you been so down this past month?"

"You're not mine to confide in anymore," she says, and when she meets my gaze, I swear water pools in her eyes before she turns her back to me. The words pierce my heart like they did when she told me something similiar a month ago. How do I make her see that it's not true? I am hers. I—

The thought captures my attention, but Emma Jane continues talking in a rushed yet unsure tone. "I'm fine, really. I've just been doing a lot of self-reflection. You know, about perfectionism and telling myself that I'm not the reason my mom died and stuff. Just reflecting on my life."

I maneuver around to stand in front of her again, placing my hand on her forearm for comfort. Her head is cast down, but I stare intently at her anyway, ducking down to try and get her attention. "Janie, I am always here for you, okay? Don't you know that by now?" *I am yours. I don't know what to do about it, but I am yours.*

After a beat of silence, she looks up at me through long eyelashes, a single tear running down her cheek. My heart breaks, and I reach to catch the liquid drop before it can fall. My finger trails up her cheek, and flames ignite in my stomach.

Seeing her cry is equivalent to getting punched in the gut.

This woman. I—

It hits me like a tidal wave, crashing over my being and giving my life new meaning.

I—*I love her.*

I love Emma Jane with every fiber of my being.

Stepping back, I drop my hand into a fist at my side. How did I not realize this sooner? All those feelings I've battled for her on and off over the past couple of years, the ones I've fought daily as of late... It is so much more than attraction. I know her. She is a smart and calculated perfectionist who has an ego the size of Texas, but... no. That's not entirely accurate.

Just like Cami, Emma Jane has been wearing a mask. One that I should have seen through. She has so much love for the people of this town in her heart that she doesn't want to ever disappoint them. So instead of allowing herself to mess up and show negative emotion, she tucks it all down. Deep down. So that no one has to worry about her. And it makes her come off as a little manipulative.

And maybe she is, but I know her heart. Her actions are never out of malice.

Something is clawing its way up, and it's tearing her apart. Is it those realizations? Is that what she's reflecting on?

Why didn't I see her sooner?

I have to tell her I'm not taken. I need to free myself to be there for her.

"Emma Jane. Mallory and I, it's—"

"I've got to go, Knightley." She walks backward, her eyes boring into my soul as she leaves. Everything within me wants to stop her.

Hug her. Kiss her. Tell her it's going to be okay and that I'm not going anywhere.

"Emma!"

She turns her back to me, grabbing her long, flowy white skirt at the sides with both hands. My heart shudders to a stop. She picks up her pace. I kick the edge of the tent before running a hand through my hair, releasing a frustrated breath. People have started looking, so I school my expression as best as I can, which means I probably look like I've been sucking on a lemon.

"It's fake," I whisper, wishing she would have stuck around to hear it.

Just get through this campaign, and then maybe...

"Hey, Knightley!" I whip around to see Mallory approaching me. She waves at Emma Jane as she passes her, but Emma Jane only nods once in greeting before continuing across the town square area full of dead grass and bare trees and people taking down their stands.

"Hey, Mallory." My voice is rough, as if I'm on the verge of crying myself. I swallow then try again. "You made it."

She tucks a strand of brown hair behind her ear before running her hands down her orange dress. "I want to call off our fake relationship."

I'm stunned silent, my mouth opening to say something but closing because I don't know what to say. She takes advantage of the silence. "You see, I've met someone. Well, it's an old friend from high school. We reconnected online, and I told him my relationship with you was for publicity purposes only. He doesn't feel new, you know? You felt new, and I wasn't ready. But with him... I think I could be ready for him. I really like him, and—"

"Let's end it," I interrupt, saying the only thing I could possibly say at the moment. *Thank you, God, for this opportunity. I don't deserve it, but thank you for Your grace.* She grins, her eyes crinkling in the corners.

"You're seriously okay with that?"

I nod, matching her smile. "Absolutely. I wish you and this guy all the happiness in the world."

"Can I still work on your team?"

"I wouldn't have it any other way, Mallory." I reach out to shake her hand.

She pulls me into a hug instead, whispering in my ear. "Go get her, okay? Don't let the age gap or fear of what people may say get in your way. I'll work on press releases to put out when you decide to announce your relationship."

Emma Jane

Rule #16: At the end of the day, encourage your clients to stay true to who they are.

If a racoon and a porcupine had a baby, it would look like my face.

I couldn't control the tears that spilled from me as I left Knightley to finish tearing down his tent by himself.

Well, with Mallory's help. I couldn't even bring myself to smile as I passed her. I'm sure they are almost finished and will head to their date night soon.

All while I sit in my car and cry.

I'm at the city park, stationed under a shady tree because I didn't want to drive home through my tears. But I also couldn't stay in the town square parking lot.

Over the past month, I've tried my hardest to accept his relationship and move on. But every time I'm in his presence, I fall more in love with him. I don't know if I'm more attracted to him when he bickers with me or when he is trying to comfort me like earlier.

I can't be attracted to him, though. He's not mine, and every time I remind myself of that, more tears start to fall.

Not that he'd want me anyway, but still.

I wanted desperately to open up to him about this past month of praying, going to the Lord, and talking to Henrietta about my issues. Of trying to overcome my excessive need to be seen as perfect. To overcome the guilt I feel over my mother's death.

I even opened up to Papa about it, and he pulled me into a hug and apologized for not talking to me about her much sooner. We spent the entire evening together a week ago, and he told me all about her. I was brought to tears over how much my mom and I have in common. Outside of our looks, we were both business-minded, wanted to benefit our communities, and, of course, suffered from PCOS. When I told Papa that I had been diagnosed at fifteen, that led to another round of apologies and tears on both of our ends. He promised me he would do everything he could to make sure I got the best treatment moving forward.

Halle has helped me just as much as Henrietta has over the past month. Both ladies have reminded me when we were out in public that it was okay if I wasn't smiling at everyone. She reminded me that I can make and keep friends by being myself, though I'm slowly figuring out who I am. I still love fashion, my job, puzzles, and games, but I no longer feel the need to be in charge of everything. I'm learning to let things fall as they may. God is constantly reminding me that I am not Him.

Mrs. Bates apologized to me, and I apologized to her. It was a sweet moment, and it has helped release the need to be perfect. At least partly. There are still moments when I succumb to the way I've been living for the past twenty-three years.

I want to tell Knightley all of this, but he's not mine to tell. He can't be the one to bring me comfort. I pick up my phone to call Halle since she knows about my feelings for Knightley, but my phone begins buzzing in my hand with a call from the man himself.

Waiting until the last possible moment to pick up, I clear my throat and answer. "Hi. What's up?" Super casual. I haven't been crying for the past fifteen minutes. Nope.

"Mallory and I broke up. Would you care to join me at The Flats for dinner?"

My gasp catches in my throat, and I have the overwhelming urge to screech at the top of my lungs like a crazed banshee. Do a victory dance. Stand on the winner's podium at the Olympics. Bees swarm in my stomach, my head explodes with fireworks, and electricity dances through my nervous system. *He's free...*

He's mine.

Slow your roll, Emma Jane. Consent is important.

"I'm so sorry, Knightley." Can he hear my broad smile?

He clears his throat. "All is well. So, will you join me?"

"Yes," I say a little too emphatically. "What time?"

Why is he calling me? Why is he inviting me to join him?

Oh, who cares!

Does this mean what I think—*hope*—it means?

"In thirty minutes. See you there, Emma." He hangs up, and I continue to hold the phone to my ear, mouth agape. The way he one-names me sends those bees in my stomach to start stinging again. My body is numb from their venom, and—

"I have to fix my makeup!" I shout to myself. I dig in my white purse, hunting for my on-the-go makeup bag. Once I've made myself presentable, I start the car and drive over to The Flats. I'm fifteen minutes early, but that's good. I have time to collect myself and try to tame this ridiculous smile that hasn't left my face since Knightley told me the news.

I take a deep breath, reminding myself that just because he's single doesn't mean he's going to date me. It doesn't mean he loves me as anything other than a sister or friend.

But at the very least, I don't feel guilty for finding him attractive and loving him as something more. And I can talk to him again. Like old times.

A knock at my window causes me to jump, and I look over to see Knightley. His blue eyes dance under the setting sun. I know I should wave or get out of my car or something, but I sit there, staring into his eyes. A small smile tugs at the corner of his lips, and I suddenly want to cup his face in my hand. Feel his beard beneath my palm. With just that little announcement that he's now available, my world has shifted.

I have to try.

Like his mother once told me, I have to at least let him know that I am an option.

He places his hand on the window, and for some reason, I bring mine up to match his. I think I can feel the heat through the glass, but that could also be my brain running haywire. When his middle finger slides down as if he was touching my hand, goosebumps ripple down my arms. The phantom touch speaks in a language I haven't yet discovered with Knightley. I yank my hand away, willing my face to cool as I start to get out of the door. He grabs the door and continues to open it as I get out, and I duck under his arm.

When he closes the door, the sound is like a warning call.

A sense of finality settles over my soul.

"Hi," he says, breathing out the word. He changed out of his blue jeans and polo from earlier and is now wearing black dress pants with a white, tucked-in button-down.

He matches me.

Was that intentional, or...? *Calm your brain, Emma Jane!*

"Ready to go inside?" he asks, and I realize I never said hello.

I shake my head. "Hi, yes. I'll follow you."

Why am I acting unbelievably awkward? *Get it together, Emma Jane. Just because you are practicing not being perfect doesn't mean you should turn into a lovestruck mess of a woman.*

We walk down the cobblestone path to the restaurant. It has floor-to-ceiling windows but we can't see inside. An outdoor chandelier hangs above the entranceway, and ivy climbs up the old brick wall around the glass door. It's a beautiful place.

Romantic.

I glance up at Knightley as I pass him to walk through the open door. A serious expression replaces the playfulness of moments earlier, and for the first time, I wonder if he's okay. Did losing Mallory genuinely hurt him even though the relationship was barely over a month-long?

Once we are seated—and I've admired the beautiful golden trim of the restaurant, the crystal lights creating a soft, warm glow, and the adequate spacing between tables that many restaurants don't pay attention to—I fix my attention fully on the handsome man sitting across from me.

"Hi," he says again, this time with a deeper, rougher tone.

Mine is the opposite as I squeak out, "Hi." I collect my composure before I speak again. "Are you okay? What happened?"

He releases a breath, red crawling up his face. His blue eyes turn pleading as he fiddles with the white tablecloth. "I have a confession, Emma Jane. You have every right to be upset with me. I'm so sorry."

A million possibilities flicker through my head as he talks, but nothing compares to his blurted truth.

"You were fake dating Mallory this entire time?" My voice is loud, struck with disbelief. He shushes me while glancing nervously around the quiet restaurant. I cover my mouth. "Oops." I should be mad. I should lay into him for lying to me about this. But I burst out in laughter, relief washing over me like a system cleanse. *He was never truly hers...*

What in the world was he thinking?

Never in a million years would I have pegged him to do such a radical thing. Me? Of course. Knightley? No way!

His regretful, shamed expression sends me over the edge, and I can't contain my howling laughter.

He shakes his head, glancing around at the perturbed restaurant-goers, but the way he's biting his bottom lip to keep from laughing tells me he's not upset with my reaction. Even if... I don't think I could have reacted any other way.

"You should be mad at me, not laughing at me." He hangs his head as if waiting for me to smite him.

I clear my throat, trying to speak in an authoritative tone, but it comes out in snorts. "What were you thinking, Squire? You lied to me for a month."

His sheepish expression says everything. "The election. Plus I thought you wanted to use the relationship for your business, so I didn't want to disappoint you by saying it failed. It was so stupid." He puffs out air and runs a hand through his thick hair.

"Knightley, I don't like that you lied to me about it, but also... I thought you hated my matchmaking business idea. Why would you try to help me?"

His expression softens. "Regardless of my feelings, I want to see you succeed, Janie."

My heart skips a beat, and I genuinely wonder if he called me here for something more.

Surely not...

But what if he did? That hand on the window thing earlier... Whew. Friends don't do that with other friends.

"You know, the fake dating thing. It's something I would do," I jest, trying to bring us to a place I'm familiar with.

He laughs. "Exactly."

"And then you would tell me," I clear my throat and prepare to do my best impersonation of Knightley, "Emma Jane, what were you thinking? You could have ended up with a psychopath. Senseless woman. Use your brain, Janie. Just a little common sense would—"

"Do I really speak to you that way?" Hurt flashes across his eyes. I drop my hands from pointing at my head (yes, I had to use my hands to speak because Knightley always does that).

"It's not a bad thing," I hurriedly say. "You're just looking out for me, that's all."

He shakes his head, a strand of red hair falling in front of his eyes. "No, that's not okay. I shouldn't talk to you like you're a petulant child incapable of making your own decisions." He pauses then says, "I'm sorry, Emma Jane."

"It's okay, really." I have the urge to reach out and take his resting hand into my own, but I don't. "I'm glad to know you care enough to set me straight at times."

"Like when you decide you want to play matchmaker with the town of Hartfield? Or, do you remember that time when you had the bright idea to turn your backyard into a field for horses? Oh, you were so scared when Henry brought those two horses home. You wouldn't even approach them from the opposite side of the fence."

"Hey! Those creatures are much larger in real life than on the internet." I wish I could say this happened when I was a kid, but sadly, this took place only two years ago. But I did end up petting the horses before we sold them. I even rode one once. "I faced my fears. You stayed by my side as you walked me right up to the horses. You held my wrist as I pet it for the first time. And then you held the reins as we went for a slow ride around the yard."

"I did, didn't I?" His gaze is far away, and I wonder if he recalls the way I clung to him for dear life after I got off the horse.

At that moment, the waiter arrives to take our orders. Once we finish ordering, Knightley excuses himself to the restroom. I take the opportunity to check my socials and text messages. My boss calls, and since Knightley isn't back, I answer.

"Hey, Mr. Sam."

"Emma Jane. Sorry to call you this late in the evening, but I just got the paperwork gathered and couldn't wait another moment to ask you a very important question."

"What is it?"

"Could you meet me in about an hour at Books and Beans?"

Knightley approaches the table, and I suddenly want to call this impromptu dinner between us a date.

"I'm actually—"

"Great. I'll see you then." He hangs up, and I breathe a laugh right as Knightley pulls his chair out to sit.

"Mr. Sam just called and asked to see me in an hour at Books and Beans," I inform him. "He said he has a question to ask me that can't wait."

"Well, we will eat quickly and meet him." Knightley sips his water as if it's settled, and those gnarly bees from earlier return.

"You're coming with me?"

He winks. "Of course. What if he's a psychopath and is luring you to murder you? I'm supposed to protect you from such beings, right?"

"Mr. Sam is far from a psychopath," I begin to argue, but then I realize what he's doing. "Nope. Back to the topic at hand. You went and got yourself a fake girlfriend. I want to hear everything."

He groans dramatically, throwing his head back and hands up. "Fine. Anything for you, Janie." As he begins to recount how and why he and Mallory created their ruse, my brain short circuits, replaying 'Anything for you, Janie' on an endless loop.

What did someone slip into my water?

KNIGHTLEY

RULE #17: LISTEN TO YOUR CLIENTS' WISHES AND DESIRES. WHETHER YOU BELIEVE IT OR NOT, THEY KNOW THEMSELVES BETTER THAN YOU KNOW THEM.

The lights inside of Books and Beans are on, but the closed sign is hanging on the door. An elderly man hobbles from around the coffee bar and gets the door for us.

"Emma Jane," he says though his eyes cut to me. "You brought your mayor friend?"

She laughs and taps my forearm. "We were having dinner when you called, so I brought him along."

"Very well," Mr. Sam says, motioning for us to follow him inside. "I've made some tea for us, but it looks like I'll need to make one more cup."

Emma Jane tells him to go ahead and sit, saying she will make a cup for me. Once we are all sitting at the center table of the cafe, Mr. Sam sighs. "I opened this cafe with my wife many years ago. She wanted to create a place where people could connect. A place for friends to gather and for business deals to take place. A place for strangers to meet and for introverts to escape to within the pages of a book." He pauses, his brown eyes flicking between me and Emma Jane. "A place for lovers to come together."

My eyes drift to Emma Jane, and she's looking at me. Not with an uncomfortable expression, but with…

Want. Desire.

Could she possibly…?

She came out to dinner with me. Dare I get my hopes up?

"We always thought I'd be the one to go first, you know?"

"Why is that?" Emma Jane asks, her attention turning back to the elderly man.

He chuckles. "She was fifteen years younger than me. Not once did I think I would outlive her, and well, I wish that wasn't the case."

I catch her gaze again, and that same expression—curious eyes, parted lips, and a slight tilt of the head—has me thinking thoughts I have no business thinking.

Or…can I have those thoughts? Mom seems to not mind us together if all of her little comments about us over the past year mean anything. Mallory encouraged me, though I had no inkling she knew about my unsolicited feelings toward Emma Jane. I will have to ask her about that later.

"I wish I could have known her," Emma Jane says, clearing her throat. She's still looking at me, however. "Ask her how she navigated falling for an older man."

Did she just—

Breath leaves my body as I process her words. Emma Jane and Mr. Sam continue talking, and I tune back into the conversation just in time to hear him offer her the business at no cost.

"I've thought about your request to purchase Books and Beans, and I prayed over whether to sell or not. But God gave me a clear answer to give this place to you and move to be with my daughter. She's pregnant, and I want to be closer to my grandchild. It is time to let this place go." Mr. Sam smiles softly, crinkles forming around his eyes. Emma Jane leaps up and accepts the offer with a tearful hug while I try to make sense of this random act of kindness.

"What just happened?" My brain is loading, catching up. When they both give me their attention—Mr. Sam nods and Emma Jane grins ear-to-ear—I say, "This is amazing, Emma Jane."

She eyes me warily, wiping a falling tear. "You aren't going to say I'm in over my head? Tell me I'm not cut out for business ownership?"

I shake my head, clearing the fog. "Not at all. You are cut out for this type of business ownership. You will do amazing things here. Matchmaking, yes, I was doubtful. But this... This was meant for you, Janie."

More tears spill from her eyes and she hugs me. I hold her tight. She feels fragile in my arms, but oh so warm and soft. Against my ear, she whispers, "Thank you, Knightley."

He goes over paperwork with her, and I review it to make sure there are no loopholes in the contracts. It's not that I don't trust Mr. Sam, but I want to protect Emma Jane at all costs.

After thirty minutes or so, I'm escorting her out of her new building and saying goodbye to Mr. Sam. Once he drives off, we look at each other and laugh.

"I can't believe I own Books and Beans now." Her incredulous expression is adorable, and without thinking, I lift her into my arms and spin her around. When I lower her to the ground, she doesn't release her arms from around my neck, so I don't drop my hands from her hips.

We stare into each other's eyes, and it's as if we are asking a million questions.

Is this okay?

Do you feel the same way?

Can we do this?

Is this weird?

Yes. Yes. Yes. And no.

In fact, it's anything but weird. She is fresh air and a feisty spirit to my calm and collected one.

I'm pulled toward her lips as if an invisible string is tugging us together, but right before I make contact, she steps away.

"Knightley, there are things you don't know."

"Like what?"

She takes my hand, and I thread my fingers between hers, following her as she leads us down the sidewalk. She doesn't talk until we turn off the main road and head toward one of the town's little nature trails.

We arrive at a bench, and she drops my hand and sits. "I can't get married, Knightley. I—"

I take her hand, cupping it between both of mine. She pegs me with a sharp stare, then casts her gaze down to her black boots. "Tell me, Janie."

"I have PCOS. My mother had it, too, apparently. I was having a flare that day you came into my room thinking I was sick. I most likely can't have kids. Even if I did get pregnant, it would be high risk. So I can't get married because I can't give a man children. Plus, there's my father."

My thumb mindlessly sweeps against the underside of her wrist as I process her words. The wind picks up, and she shivers. I curse under my breath, wishing I had a jacket with me. Instead, I wrap my arms around her, acting as a shield against the wind. She smells of sweetness and...

Home.

Forget the jacket. This is a thousand times better. She leans her head against my shoulder, her shoulders rising and falling with light sobs.

When she finally sits back and looks at me with her tearful eyes, I bring my hand to her cheek. "Janie, do not associate your marital worth with your childbearing capabilities."

She nods her head, but she's still not smiling.

"Why are you just now telling me this?" I ask.

Her glistening gray eyes flick to my lips, and it takes everything within me not to kiss her. Now is not the time. Not when she's feeling so invaluable.

"Knightley," her eyes move back up my face, "do you—" She pauses, releasing a sigh. "Do you think—"

She shakes her head, a laugh of disbelief passing through her lips.

I hook my finger under her chin, forcing her to meet my gaze. "Emma, I want you to know that you are the most precious woman in my life. Any man would be a fool to not want to marry you if that is something you choose to do."

"Including you?" she asks, and I nod, not trusting myself to speak.

After a moment, I stand and grab her hand. "Let's start heading back to our vehicles before it gets any later."

We walk in companionable silence, though a million unspoken declarations and questions hang above our head.

It's time I face the facts.

Emma Jane wants something more with me. Do her feelings run as deep as mine? By her little marriage comment, I'm hopeful, but also, she could have just been teasing me or seeking validation in her fragile state.

Whatever it may be, it's time to find out.

We reach our vehicles, and I open her car door as she stands unmoving beside me.

Before I realize what's happening, she rises to her tiptoes, places a hand on my shoulder, and kisses my cheek. She ducks under my arm and slides into her car, shutting the door. I'm stunned as she drives off, my hand mindlessly rubbing the heated spot on my face.

Emma Jane

Rule #18: Encourage direct actions. Words aren't always enough.

The new reverend is an elderly gentleman with a pleasant smile and a warm aura. Overall, I think he will make the congregation feel at ease after the sleazy Elton Philip.

"Knightley's single now, did you hear?" Henrietta's voice causes me to jump, but when I turn to face her, she's wearing a smirk. "Are you going to tell him how you feel?"

I think of last night. Of kissing his cheek before I left.

I all but told him I'd marry him, and I'm not sure exactly where that came from other than the murky depths of my soul.

Because it's true.

I more than like Knightley.

I'm in love with him.

After he encouraged me to take over Books and Beans, I knew I wanted him by my side for the entire process. For the rest of my life. And I think he feels the same way.

"I want to," I say, looking over Knightley. He's talking with Marcus, and when he sneaks a glance my way, his smile broadens. I can't help but smile in return. We did that for the entire church service. He sat in the row across from me, and we kept catching each other stealing glances.

Knightley is rocking plaid pants again, and when he starts walking my way (I haven't lifted my eyes from the way his thighs look in those bad boys), my breath hitches and my heartbeat picks up. Henrietta shoves me toward him, and I all but stumble into his arms.

"Easy there, Janie."

I glare back at Henrietta. "It was my so-called friend."

He laughs then takes my hand.

In front of everyone!

Something has definitely shifted.

"I'm stealing you away for lunch. Is that okay?" But he's already pulling me behind him toward his truck.

"By all means," I say in a mock exasperated manner through girlish giggles.

Once we are inside his truck, we drive in mutual silence to the nearest grocery store.

"I'll be quick. Stay here."

"Grab a water for me, please," I call as he shuts the door.

Fifteen minutes later, he's back in the truck with two armfuls of grocery bags.

"Here's your water." He tosses it to me from the back seat where he's setting down everything he bought.

"What's going on?" I ask, eyeing the folded black outdoor blanket.

"We are going on a picnic."

"What? Where?"

He chuckles as he cranks the truck back up. "Down to the lake behind your house."

We once more fall into silence as he drives, but my nerves are popping. He hasn't stopped smiling this entire drive—from the church to the store and now to the lake. What is he doing? Why do I feel like a bundle of nerves?

But also, I feel settled. Whole. Complete as a finished puzzle.

I'm going to tell him. I don't know why he wants to take me on a picnic, but I pray it's because he feels the same way I do. All the signs are there. The feeling of something new is in the air.

I'm going to woman-up and tell him that I love him.

Okay, maybe I'll start by saying I like him. As more than a friend. Make sure I don't scare him off in case I've been reading everything wrong.

We arrive at the lake, and the sun reflects brightly off the water, causing diamonds to sparkle across the top of the surface. There is a light breeze, and the bracing autumn air is perfect.

I help him unload everything, and he talks me through all the foods he bought. Meats, cheeses, fruits, crackers, and chocolates. A wonderful combination.

After everything is set up, there's nothing left to do but sit down and eat.

And talk...

I clear my throat, trying to be brave. "Why did you bring me out here for a picnic, Knightley?"

He stops mid-bite of a meat and cheese cracker. "I just thought it'd be nice. It's a beautiful day, and I wanted to make sure we were okay from yesterday."

He's rambling, so I stand.

"What are you doing?" he asks, but when I walk a few steps over to the tree, he stands and follows.

Taking a deep breath, I decide it's now or never.

I've never been one to back down from something I want, and I want Knightley George Austen. And judging by everything that happened last night and this random picnic, I think he wants me, too.

I plant my palms against his chest, heat burning through the thin, green fabric, and I shove him against the tree.

"Emma Jane. What in the world are you doing?" Knightley's chest heaves underneath my palms, his back against the tree as red tints his pale, freckled face. Wild blue eyes stare at me like saucers awaiting a cup of tea. His hands are pressed against the oak, and I don't miss the way his long fingers strain as if he's gripping the bark to keep from grabbing something else.

Someone else.

Me.

"What you won't do." I stretch to my tiptoes, squeezing my eyes closed and taking the biggest matchmaking risk of my life. The last one of this stupid business I plan to dissolve. The moment my lips should be colliding with his, I'm met with...

Beard hair.

Infiltrating my mouth and poking my nose.

I open my eyes to a blurry vision of red hair, then I take a small step backward. "Did you just block me from kissing you?"

"Pray tell, Emma. Why are you trying to kiss me?" Knightley's voice is tainted with a gravelly rasp.

"Because I'm pretty sure you like me the way I like you. And I do mean as much more than family friends, Squire."

He swallows, shifting his eyes away from my lips. "Janie, you're thirteen years younger than me."

His hands release the tree bark and fall to his side.

"So?"

"You want an old codger like myself?"

His fingers twitch at his side as his head, ever so subtly, tilts toward me.

"I'm a grown woman, Knightley. I can choose who I want."

"And you want me? You truly want me?"

"I do."

He sighs as if every piece of his puzzle is falling into place. "How did I not see you sooner, Janie?" Knightley's breath washes over my face, minty and uniquely him. He moves his hand to my face, his thumb swiping across my bottom lip. "Are you positive?"

"I tried to kiss you. Of course, I'm positive. I started this."

He closes his eyes. "And you want me to finish it?"

I let out a breathy, victorious yes, my eyelids fluttering closed, the afternoon sun fading from view.

"I love you, Emma Jane Williams. What I feel, it's more than simply *liking* you. Words can't do my feelings justice. You are charmingly selfish, beautifully calculating, witty, intelligent, fun, and perfectly imperfect. If I kiss you, this is for forever. Got it? There's nothing more to say, so stop me if you're not going to marry me. Because it's you or no one for me, Janie."

My stomach leaps with excitement at his declaration, and I loop my arms around his neck, tugging lightly at the back of his hair as I grin. He's it for me, too. I never had a desire to marry because of my condition. I've never been much of a romantic.

But Knightley? He makes me want it all. And because it's him, I know he will love and accept me whether I can give him a child or not. I know he will hold my hand when I'm sad about it. I know he will remind me that my worth isn't in childbearing.

For Knightley… I will take the jump. I will choose forever. "Oh, I'm going to marry the heck out of you."

His lips press against mine, soft and cautious. He tastes of strawberry lip balm, endless possibilities, and the culmination of hope I never dared to allow myself to consider until last night when he said he'd be a fool not to marry me.

Marriage.

To Knightley Austen.

A man who's been in my life for as long as I can comprehensively remember, and even before that.

He deepens the kiss, and whereas I started this escapade, he now fully controls it. His lips dance with mine in a perfect waltz, slow and steady and sure. When he straightens, tilting my jaw up to follow him, a low rumble sounds from his chest.

Or is it mine?

Am I capable of that noise?

These feelings… They are all explosive and new. Like a puzzle, I want to piece him together just to break him apart. *In the most delicious of ways…*

I now understand why Halle said she didn't wait until marriage. We are going to have to be very careful.

Knightley bites my bottom lip, and I surrender to him until I can't remember my own name.

Finally, after what could have been centuries, he steps back, breathing heavily. I feel lighter than I have in months. And I'm exceptionally glad to report I now enjoy kissing.

He meets my eyes and a huge grin breaks across his face. "This is real?"

"It's so real." I throw my arms around his neck and drag his lips back down to mine. He loves me for all my faults. He will stand by my side as I continue to work through them all. He will call me on my crap, and I will fight him over it. He will win, and I will love every single second of it.

But then a thought breaks through my lovestruck haze. "We have to tell Papa."

KNIGHTLEY

RULE #19: DON'T FOLLOW YOUR HEART; INSTEAD, FOLLOW YOUR INTUITION. THE HOLY SPIRIT. YOUR CLIENTS DESERVE SOLID GROUND TO STAND ON, NOT A CRUMBLING FOUNDATION.

Bile rises in my throat as I knock on Henry's door.

I never knock.

Why am I knocking now?

Especially when his daughter is beside me, clutching my hand.

"Calm down, Knightley." She squeezes my hand even tighter.

I laugh, but nerves drown the sound out. "You calm down. You're cutting off circulation in my hand."

The doorknob turns, and I release Emma Jane's hand, but she doesn't release mine. Henry's tired-as-usual face graces the entrance as he gives me an odd expression. "Why are you knock—" His gaze drops to our intertwined fingers.

Well, my fingers are still frozen in mid-flex while Emma Jane is rubbing small, calming circles on my thumb.

"Oh."

At his unimpressed tone, Emma Jane and I sneak glances at one another, silently asking, "What's going on?"

"Don't just stand out here," Henry says, walking inside. "It's cold and drafty. Come inside, you two."

Perplexed, we follow him into the foyer, entering the sitting room where his fire feels good for once since it's almost Halloween.

This room is familiar but foreign. I've stepped foot in here, had tea in here, laughed in here, and have done business in here. But holding Emma Jane's hand within these four walls is not something I've ever done.

When I sit down on the settee and she slides up right next to me, our thighs pressed together so that a single piece of paper could not fit between them, I catalog the action as another new thing to happen in this room.

The silence is suffocating as Henry stares at us with a blank expression. When Emma Jane tries to speak, Henry holds up one finger, and we sit in silence for another minute.

"Henry, I can explain—"

"Do you love her, Knightley?"

His stern eyes and straightforward voice shock me. "Yes sir. I love her very much."

"Emma Jane. Do you love him?"

"Yes, Papa. I love him." She looks up at me, a huge grin overtaking her face, and I smile like a champion. She is the only thing I needed to win this election season.

"Very well. You have my blessing."

"Thank you, Henry—" I begin, but Emma Jane interrupts.

"Papa. I'm going to marry him."

He harrumphs, not bothering to look at the two of us. "I figured as much."

"If I may ask, sir. How so?"

"Because my Emma Jane wouldn't show up at the front door holding just any man's hand." He pauses, scratching his chin. "I saw the way you two looked at each other the day after Halle and Grant's wedding. I don't think either of you recognized the sparks flying. I knew a ticking clock was at play, and so I've been working on accepting this moment for a while now."

Emma Jane meets my eyes, and we both bite back joyous laughter.

For the sake of Henry, of course.

"All right, well. Go on, now. I'm sure your mother would love to hear the news, Knightley. She's been pestering me to help push you two together over the past year."

Emma Jane pops up, walks over to her father, and kisses his cheek. "You'll always be my number one man, okay, Papa?"

He grunts, but a small smile tugs at the corner of his lips. As Emma Jane leaves the room, I pat Henry's back. "I'll take good care of her, Henry."

He looks at me, still wearing a little grin. "I know you will. I wouldn't have allowed it otherwise."

"I'm so sorry, Knightley..." Emma Jane's voice trails off, her gray eyes wide with panic.

And all I can do is laugh as I stare at the newspaper headline: KNIGHTLEY CAUGHT KISSING!

I toss the paper to the side and pull Emma Jane into my arms. "I'm not the least bit sorry to be caught kissing you."

She pushes away from me, her face still showing her panic. "But there's no way you can win this election now. People are going to start calling you a predator. They don't know our story. Our history!"

"So we will tell them." I step toward her, brushing a blonde lock from her face. "And I'm going to step down from the race."

"Are you sure, Knightley? I mean, I agree. I don't see a way around this now that it's out, regardless of what we say to the people. They will go on believing what they want."

"I'm positive. I only ran in the first place because no one of quality was running. Jay will be an amazing mayor, and I can focus on my law firm, help with your business transition with Books and Beans, and, well, love you *well*." I lower my voice on that last part, bending down to kiss her neck. She smells like coconut and flowers. Pleasant and enticing. "We have a wedding to plan, anyway."

"You never actually proposed, Squire."

Chuckling, I nibble on her ear. "Soon, Janie."

I still can't believe I now have free rein to think about her in this way. To touch her. Kiss her. Feel her body shiver against mine when I whisper in her ear.

She's the only woman I'd choose to get married again for, and I'm thrilled to see what our future has in store.

"How are we going to go about this?" Her fingers run up and down my back while her other hand grips my arm.

I mumble against her neck. "I'll release a video to my social media page."

She giggles when I get to that spot behind her ear that tickles her. "Okay, okay. Enough. We need to talk about this."

Sighing, I step back, taking her hands in mine.

I can't seem to stop touching her now that I have permission to.

"What's there to talk about?"

"I want to be in your video. I want people to hear from me. I've gotten messages on my social media from people asking if I'm okay."

My eyes widen. "Do they think I'm forcing you?"

"Something like that."

"I would never do such a thing! You are a consenting adult, and—" Heated indignation rises in my throat, cutting off my speech.

Now it's Emma Jane's turn to laugh. "I know, Squire. But they don't. And that's okay. Our relationship is for us." She interlaces her fingers with mine, and that's all it takes to ground me. "We will show them that with every year that passes where we remain happy, healthy, and completely in love. This is our story. No one else's."

I lean down to kiss her neck once more. "The story of how Emma Jane made a match for the mayor..."

She giggles, gently pulling away from me before taking my face in her soft hands. Pressing her lips against mine, she mumbles, "Rule number one: don't fall for your client."

Cami

I've spent ten years wandering the earth as what some people may call a ghost or a spirit.

But I'm not a ghost.

I might be a spirit.

One thing is for sure: I'm cursed.

And I have no way to get out of this sickening in-between.

Read Cami's story in *Frosted Soul,* an urban fantasy romance coming soon by Drew Taylor

ALSO BY

Drew Taylor

Loved the story? Consider leaving a review on Goodreads and Amazon! Read on for a note regarding series tie-ins!

<3

Sign up for my newsletter where you will receive access to bonus scenes, additional chapters, extended epilogues, and much more! New content added at random!

<3

Scan the QR code or click on the link to learn more about Drew Taylor's books!

www.drewtaylorwrites.com

THE DESIGNATED SERIES

Emma Jane and Knightley first make their appearance in the *Designated* series! Emma Jane's first appearance is in *The Designated Valentine*, and Knightley's first appearance is in *The Designated Twin*. This story *(Emma Jane's Guide to Matchmaking the Mayor)* runs in tandem with events found in *The Designated Date* (Stone and Lucy's story).

ACKNOWLEDGMENTS

To my Lord and Savior, Jesus Christ. As always!

Wow, I had such a fun time writing this book! *Emma* is my favorite Jane Austen novel, and to be honest, Emma Woodhouse is one of my favorite characters of all time. She is witty, intelligent, concerned, and full of life. She's perfectly imperfect, and maybe that's what I like most about her. We are all selfish, controlling, and calculating at times. Learning how to overcome those tendencies is what is truly important. I hope I did Jane Austen justice with this short novella. I hope she'd be proud of me.

First of all, thank you to the authors who joined this collaboration with me! I had a vision of fun, light rom-coms that would correlate to the political season. You all came through! Thanks for agreeing to do this with me, and thanks for putting out amazing novellas! I want to thank my amazing critique partners (Latisha and Kim), beta readers (Cole, Ally, and Sierra), editor (Leah), and proofreader (Lindsay). You all are my author village, and I couldn't write a book without y'all! Shoutout to my best friend Whitney who is always there to chat about plots, characters, and other story elements with me. I love you more than words can explain, girly pop. To my parents and grandma—thanks for your unwavering support. Drew's Crew: you all are rays of sunshine to my soul. My books would get nowhere without your constant sharing, reviewing, and recommending. Thanks for being a part of my community.

And lastly, to all my devoted readers, THANK YOU. I can't believe you all take the time to read words I string together within the depths of my brain and transplant onto paper. How did I get so blessed? I truly don't deserve it, but I am #grateful.

ABOUT THE AUTHOR

Drew Taylor writes closed-door chick-lit romance stories from a Biblical worldview, saturating them with "Jesus glitter." She believes faith-based romance can be full of heart, humor, healing, and hope while showcasing the reality of our fallen human condition. Her redemptive and engaging love stories point to the One who embodies true love–Jesus Christ.

Drew lives in the great state of Mississippi, where she runs her company (Taylor Made Publishing, LLC) out of her bedroom. When not working or writing, she enjoys reading, baking, researching conspiracy theories, and spending quality time with the people who mean the most to her.

Follow Drew:

Instagram: @authordrewtaylor

Facebook: Drew Taylor, Author

TikTok: @drewtaylorwrites

Pinterest: @authordrewtaylor

YouTube: @authordrewtaylor